MANOSAURS

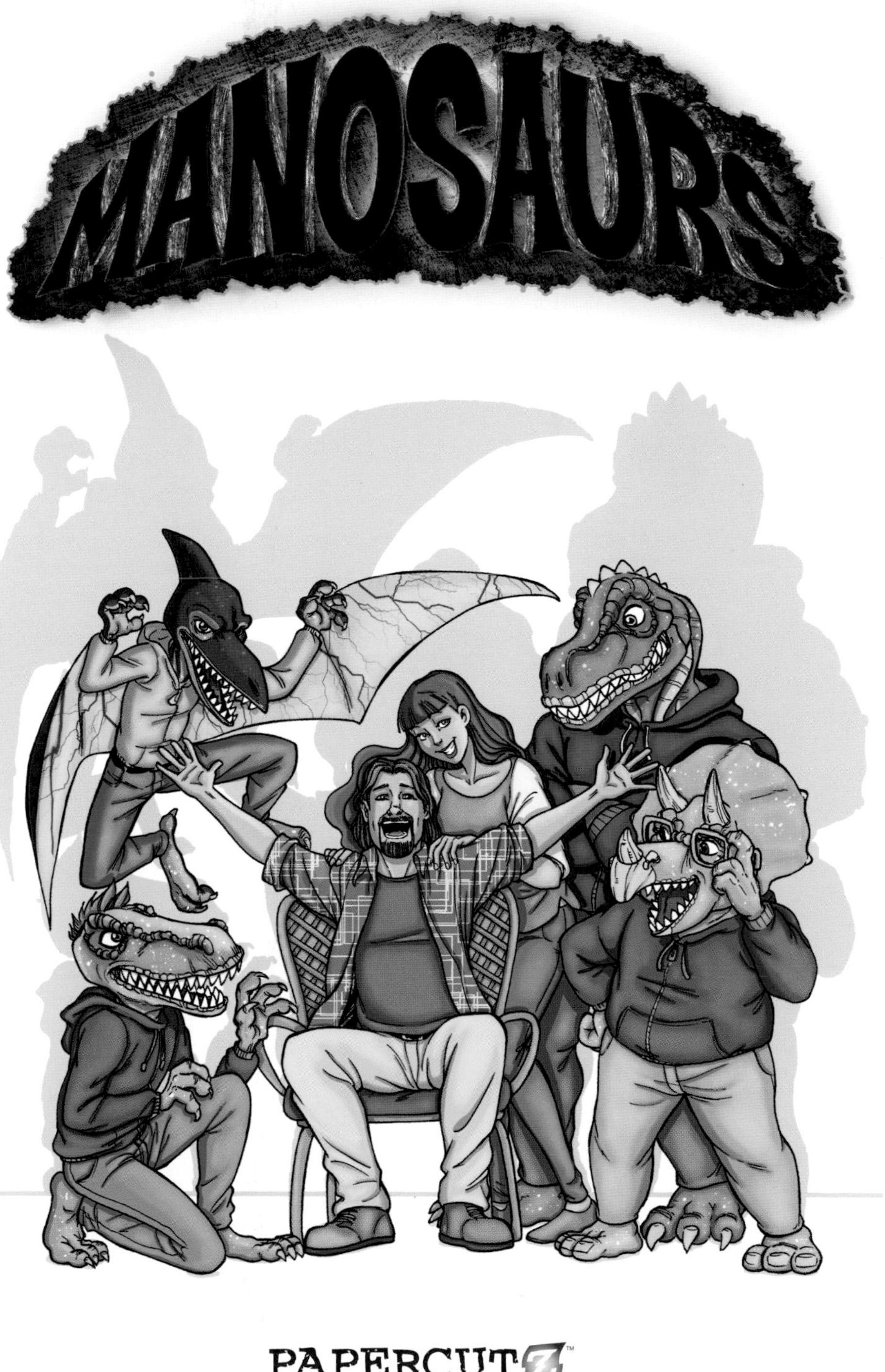

PAPERCUTZ

MORE GREAT GRAPHIC NOVEL SERIES AVAILABLE FROM PAPERCUTZ

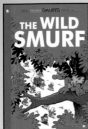

THE WILD SMURF
THE SMURFS #21

GARFIELD
APPRENTICE SORCERER
THE GARFIELD SHOW #6

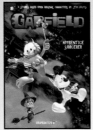

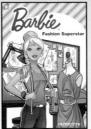

Barbie
Fashion Superstar
BARBIE #1

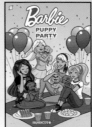

Barbie
PUPPY PARTY
BARBIE PUPPY PARTY

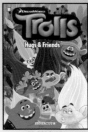

DreamWorks
Trolls
Hugs & Friends
TROLLS #1

All-new, full-color Graphic Novel
Geronimo Stilton
THE MYSTERY OF THE PIRATE SHIP
GERONIMO STILTON #17

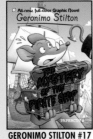

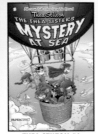

All-new, full-color Graphic Novel
Thea Stilton
THE THEA SISTERS
MYSTERY AT SEA
THEA STILTON #6

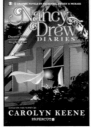

Nancy Drew
DIARIES
CAROLYN KEENE
NANCY DREW DIARIES #7

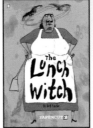

The Lunch Witch
THE LUNCH WITCH #1

Scarlett
Star on the Run
SCARLETT

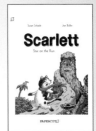

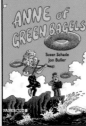

ANNE of GREEN BAGELS
Susan Schade
Jon Buller
ANNE OF GREEN BAGELS #1

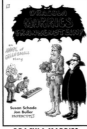

DRACULA MARRIES FRANKENSTEIN!
Susan Schade
Jon Buller
DRACULA MARRIES FRANKENSTEIN!

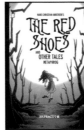

THE RED SHOES
AND OTHER TALES
METAPHROG
THE RED SHOES

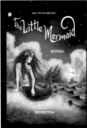

The Little Mermaid
METAPHROG
THE LITTLE MERMAID

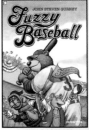

JOHN STEVEN GURNEY
Fuzzy Baseball
FUZZY BASEBALL

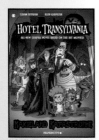

HOTEL TRANSYLVANIA
HOTEL TRANSYLVANIA #1

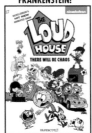

THE LOUD HOUSE
THERE WILL BE CHAOS
THE LOUD HOUSE #1

WALK LIKE A MANOSAUR!
MANOSAURS #1

THE ONLY LIVING BOY
TO SAVE A SHATTERED WORLD
THE ONLY LIVING BOY #5

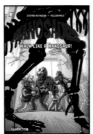

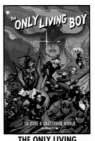

MANOSAURS

#1 "WALK LIKE A MANOSAUR!"

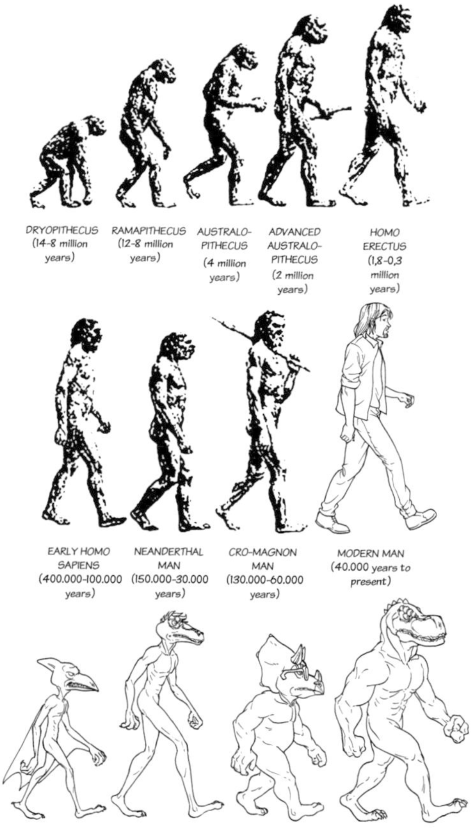
DRYOPITHECUS (14-8 million years)
RAMAPITHECUS (12-8 million years)
AUSTRALO-PITHECUS (4 million years)
ADVANCED AUSTRALO-PITHECUS (2 million years)
HOMO ERECTUS (1,8-0,3 million years)
EARLY HOMO SAPIENS (400.000-100.000 years)
NEANDERTHAL MAN (150.000-30.000 years)
CRO-MAGNON MAN (130.000-60.000 years)
MODERN MAN (40.000 years to present)

STEFAN PETRUCHA — WRITER
YELLOWHALE STUDIOS — ARTISTS
MANOSAURS CREATED BY STUART FISCHER

PAPERCUTZ™
NEW YORK

#1 "Walk Like a Manosaur!"
Inspired by the MANOSAURS comicbook series created by Stuart Fischer.
Man-Comet co-created by Stefan Petrucha and Maia Kinney-Petrucha.

Stefan Petrucha – Writer
Yellowhale Creative Studio s.r.l. - Rome/IT
Marcello De Martino – Artist
Roberta Pierpaoli – Inker
Francesca Vivaldi – Colorist
Maryam Funicelli, Dawn Guzzo – Letterers
Stefania Bitta – Studio Supervisor
MANOSAURS logo design – JayJay Jackson
Martin Satryb – Design/Production
Jeff Whitman – Assistant Managing Editor
Jim Salicrup
Editor-in-Chief

ISBN: 978-162991-813-6 paperback edition
ISBN: 978-162991-814-3 hardcover edition

Papercutz books may be purchased for business or promotional use.
For information on bulk purchases please contact Macmillan Corporate and
Premium Sales Department at (800) 221-7945 x5442.

Printed in Korea
November 2017

Distributed by Macmillan
First Printing

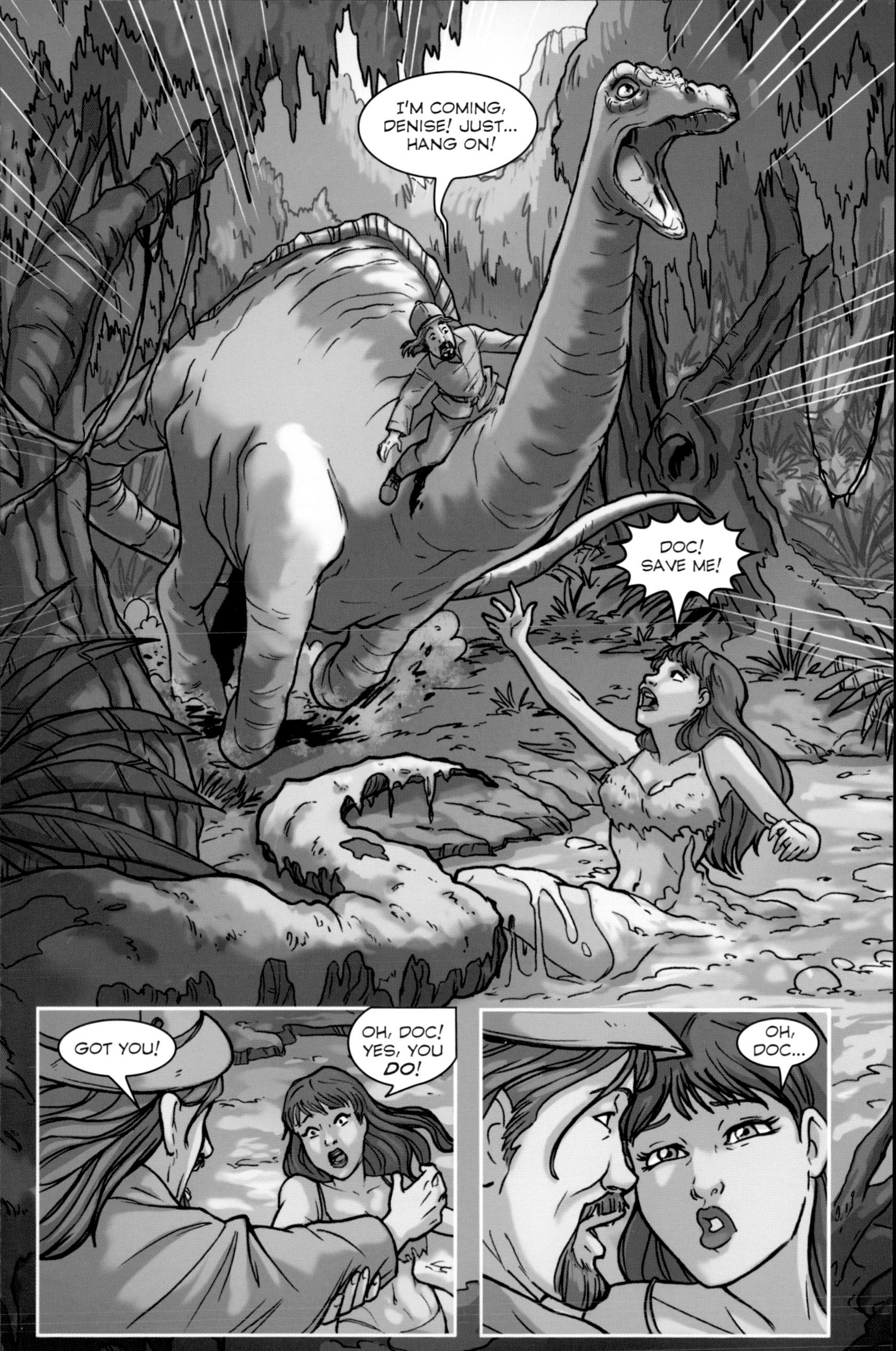
I'M COMING, DENISE! JUST... HANG ON!
DOC! SAVE ME!
GOT YOU!
OH, DOC! YES, YOU DO!
OH, DOC...

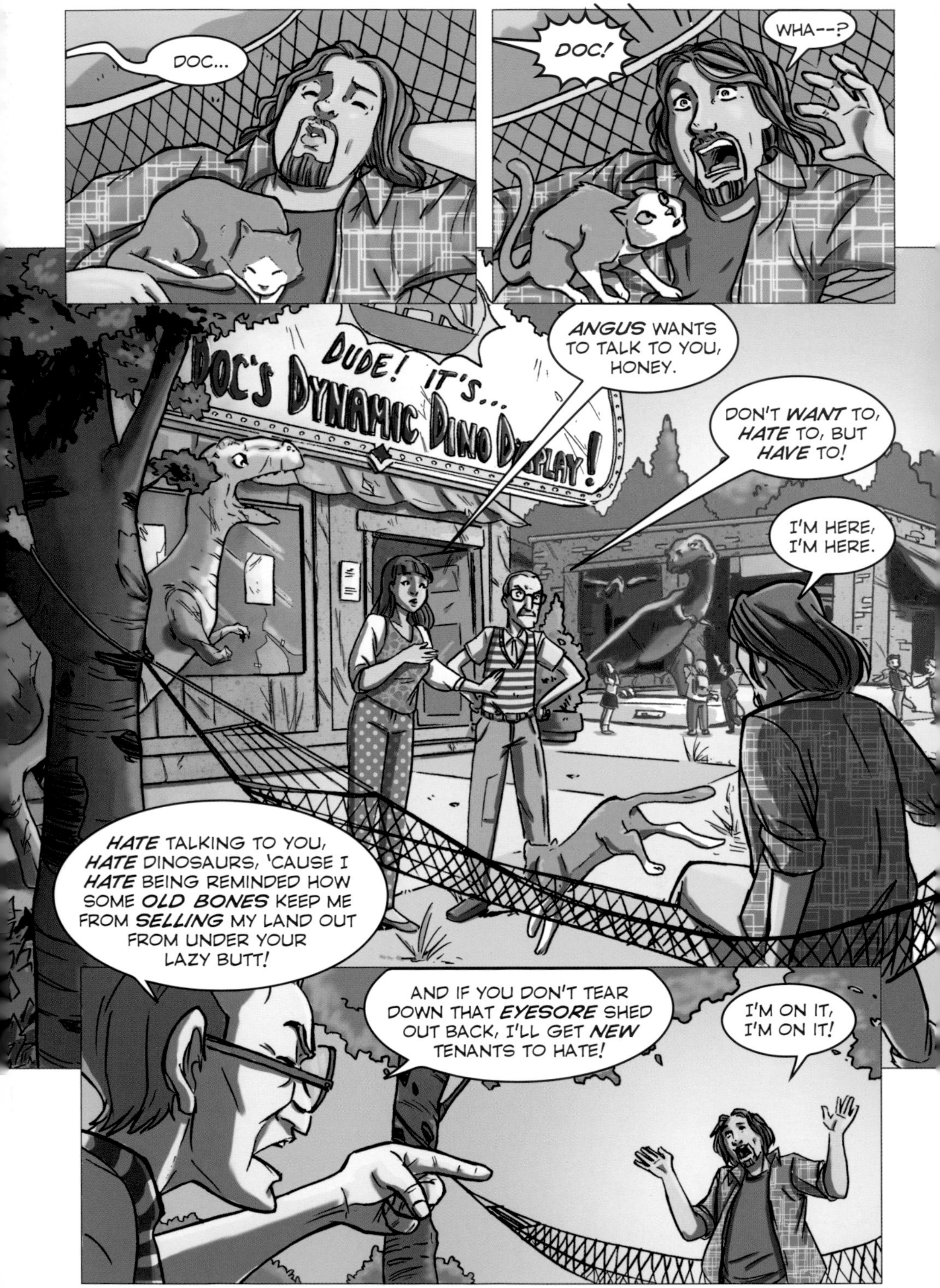
DOC...
DOC!
WHA--?
DUDE! IT'S... DOC'S DYNAMIC DINO DISPLAY!
ANGUS WANTS TO TALK TO YOU, HONEY.
DON'T WANT TO, HATE TO, BUT HAVE TO!
I'M HERE, I'M HERE.
HATE TALKING TO YOU, HATE DINOSAURS, 'CAUSE I HATE BEING REMINDED HOW SOME OLD BONES KEEP ME FROM SELLING MY LAND OUT FROM UNDER YOUR LAZY BUTT!
AND IF YOU DON'T TEAR DOWN THAT EYESORE SHED OUT BACK, I'LL GET NEW TENANTS TO HATE!
I'M ON IT, I'M ON IT!

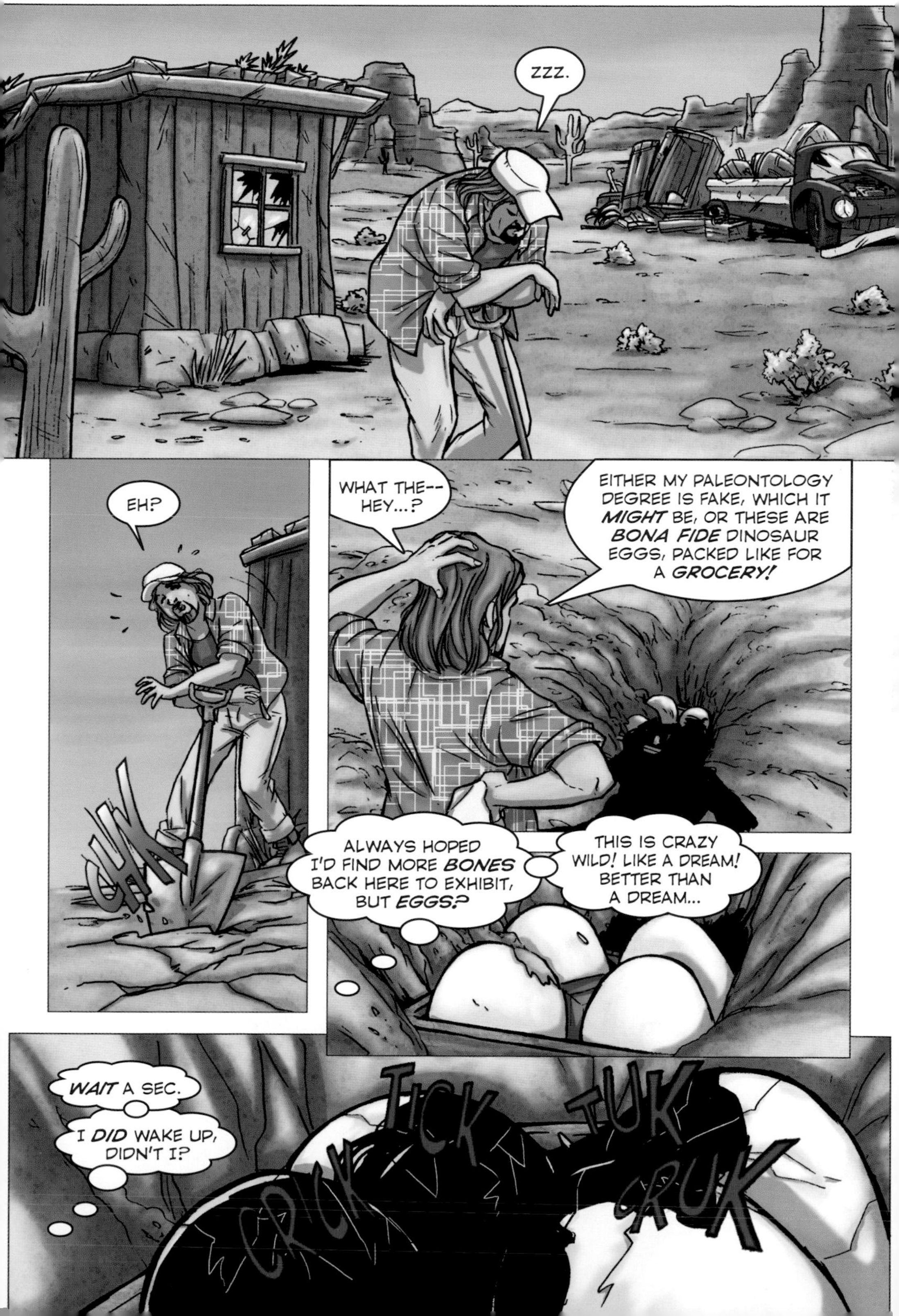
ZZZ.
EH?
CHK
WHAT THE-- HEY...?
EITHER MY PALEONTOLOGY DEGREE IS FAKE, WHICH IT MIGHT BE, OR THESE ARE BONA FIDE DINOSAUR EGGS, PACKED LIKE FOR A GROCERY!
ALWAYS HOPED I'D FIND MORE BONES BACK HERE TO EXHIBIT, BUT EGGS?
THIS IS CRAZY WILD! LIKE A DREAM! BETTER THAN A DREAM...
WAIT A SEC.
I DID WAKE UP, DIDN'T I?
TICK
TUK
CRICK
CRUK

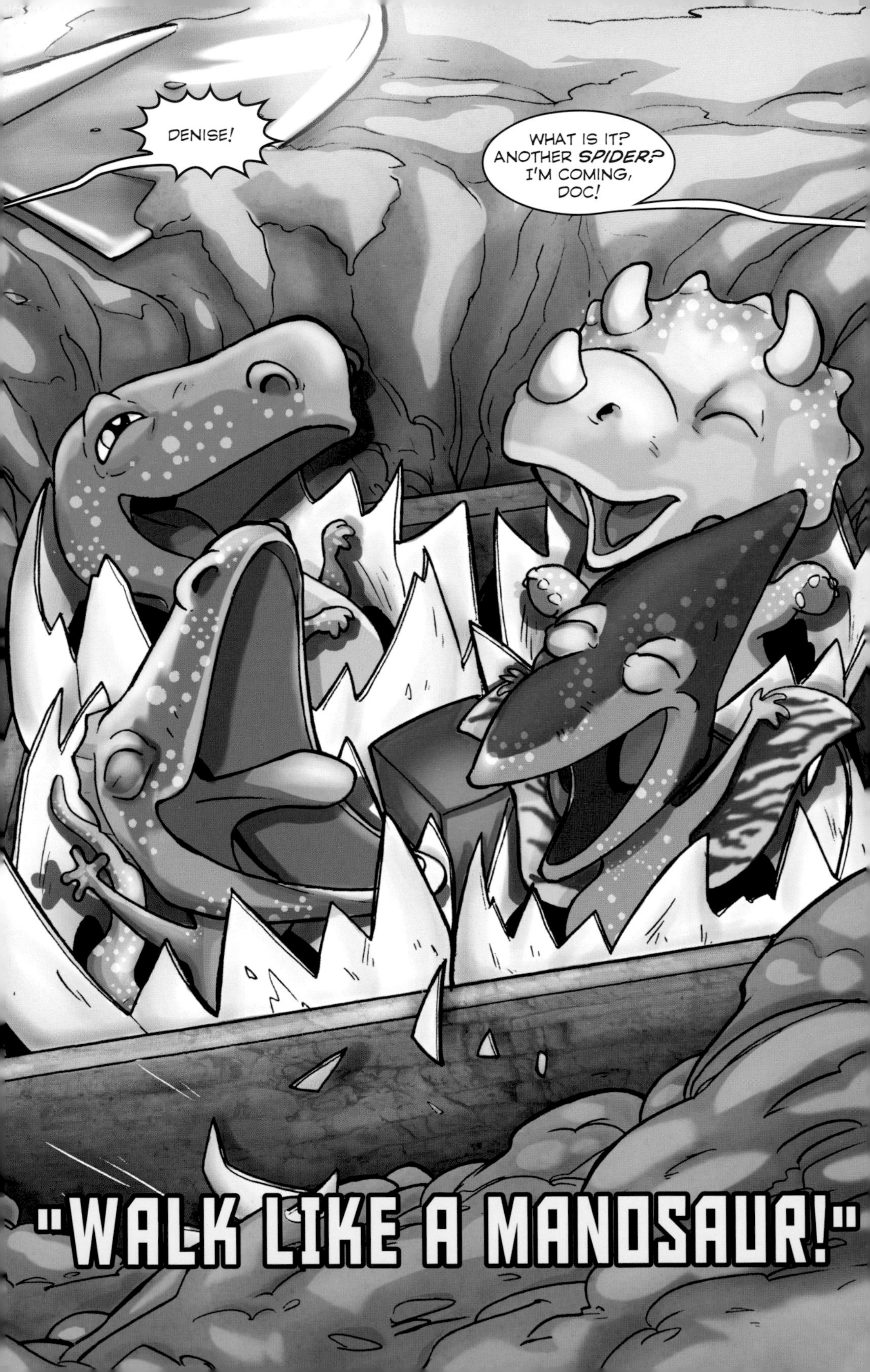
DENISE!
WHAT IS IT? ANOTHER SPIDER? I'M COMING, DOC!
"WALK LIKE A MANOSAUR!"

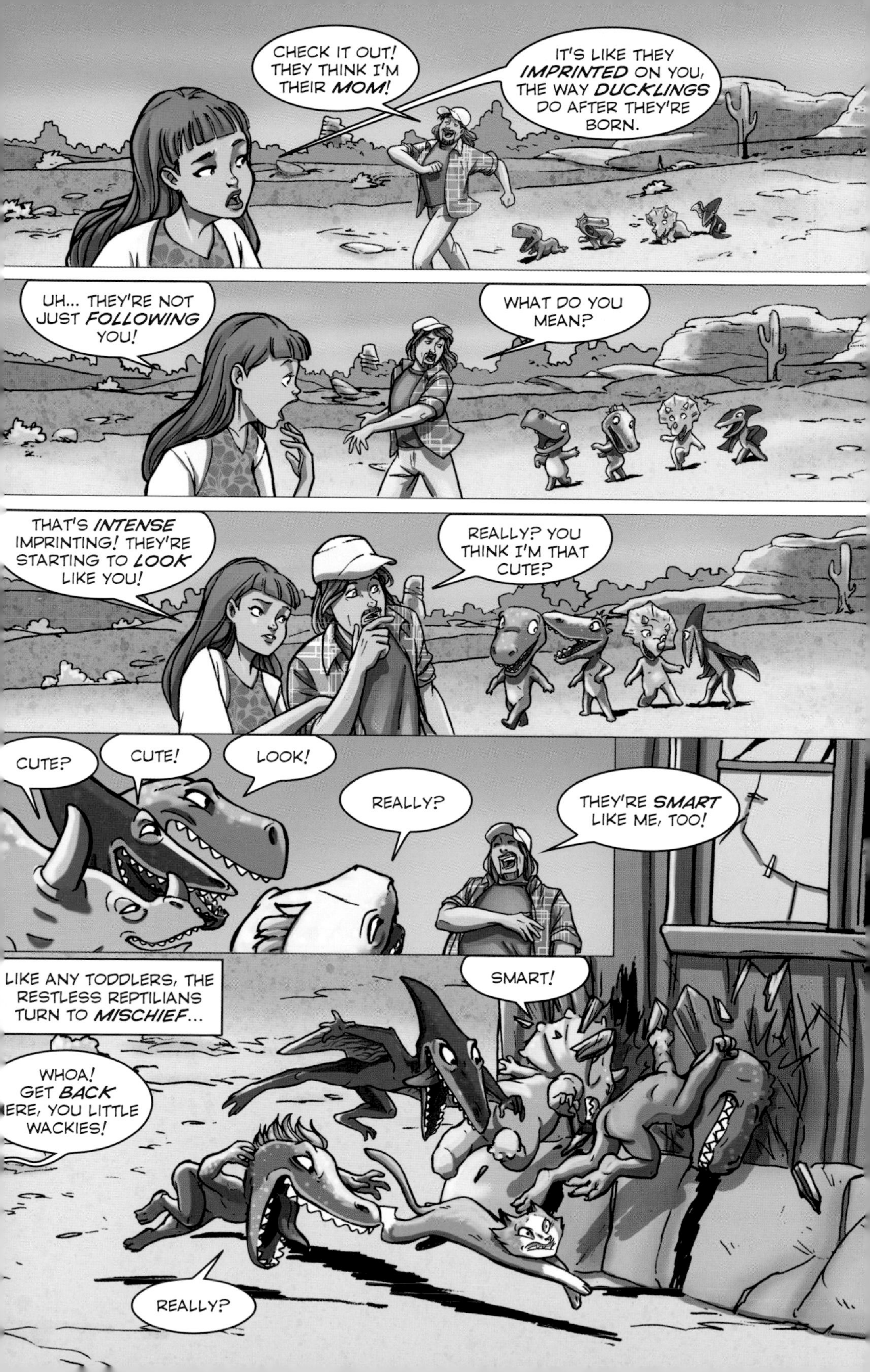
CHECK IT OUT! THEY THINK I'M THEIR MOM!
IT'S LIKE THEY IMPRINTED ON YOU, THE WAY DUCKLINGS DO AFTER THEY'RE BORN.
UH... THEY'RE NOT JUST FOLLOWING YOU!
WHAT DO YOU MEAN?
THAT'S INTENSE IMPRINTING! THEY'RE STARTING TO LOOK LIKE YOU!
REALLY? YOU THINK I'M THAT CUTE?
CUTE?
CUTE!
LOOK!
REALLY?
THEY'RE SMART LIKE ME, TOO!
LIKE ANY TODDLERS, THE RESTLESS REPTILIANS TURN TO MISCHIEF...
SMART!
WHOA! GET BACK ERE, YOU LITTLE WACKIES!
REALLY?

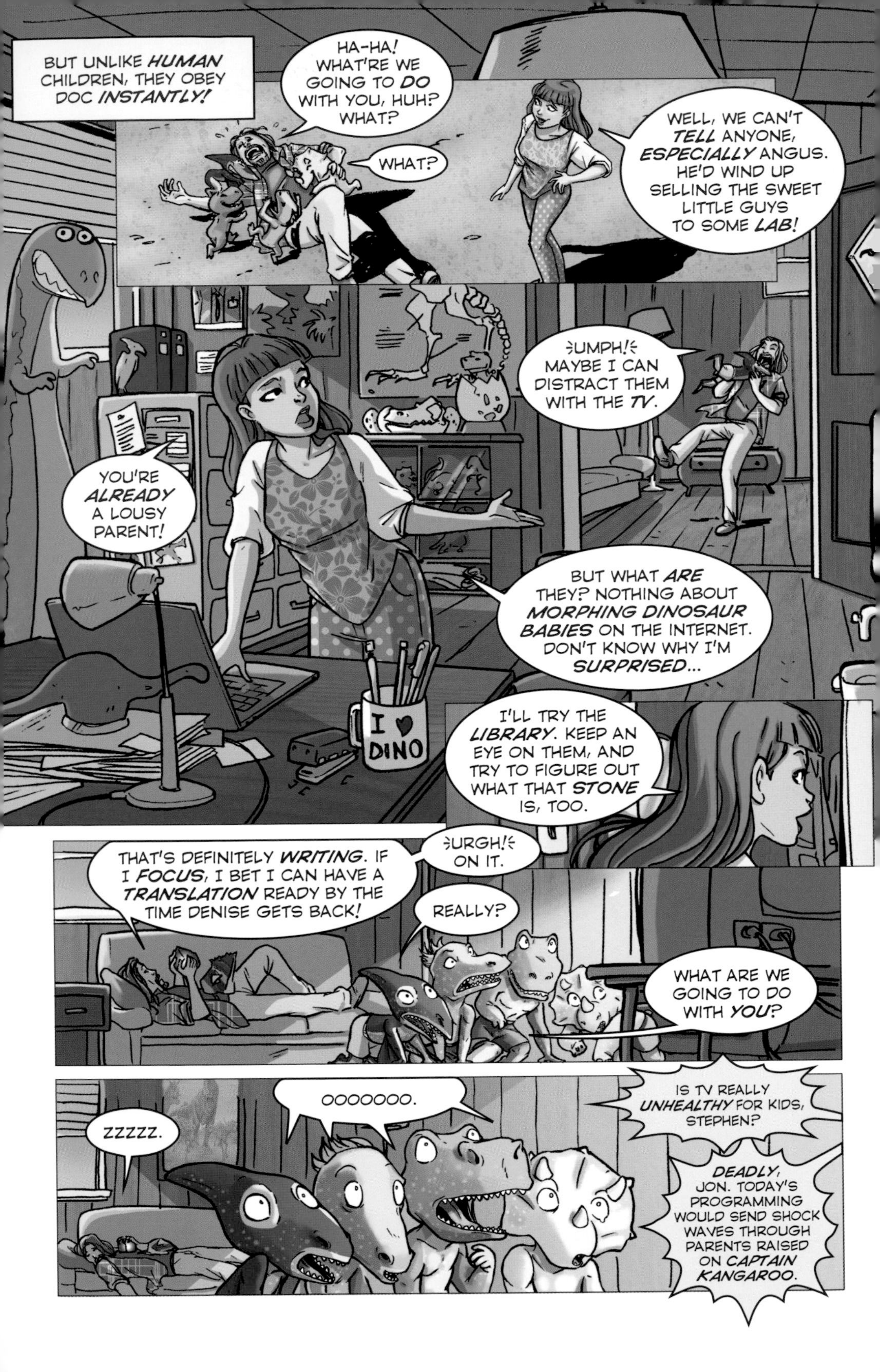
BUT UNLIKE *HUMAN* CHILDREN, THEY OBEY DOC *INSTANTLY!*
HA-HA! WHAT'RE WE GOING TO *DO* WITH YOU, HUH? WHAT?
WHAT?
WELL, WE CAN'T *TELL* ANYONE, *ESPECIALLY* ANGUS. HE'D WIND UP SELLING THE SWEET LITTLE GUYS TO SOME *LAB!*
UMPH! MAYBE I CAN DISTRACT THEM WITH THE *TV*.
YOU'RE *ALREADY* A LOUSY PARENT!
BUT WHAT *ARE* THEY? NOTHING ABOUT *MORPHING DINOSAUR BABIES* ON THE INTERNET. DON'T KNOW WHY I'M *SURPRISED*...
I ♥ DINO
I'LL TRY THE *LIBRARY*. KEEP AN EYE ON THEM, AND TRY TO FIGURE OUT WHAT THAT *STONE* IS, TOO.
URGH! ON IT.
THAT'S DEFINITELY *WRITING*. IF I *FOCUS*, I BET I CAN HAVE A *TRANSLATION* READY BY THE TIME DENISE GETS BACK!
REALLY?
WHAT ARE WE GOING TO DO WITH *YOU*?
ZZZZZ.
OOOOOOO.
IS TV REALLY *UNHEALTHY* FOR KIDS, STEPHEN?
DEADLY, JON. TODAY'S PROGRAMMING WOULD SEND SHOCK WAVES THROUGH PARENTS RAISED ON *CAPTAIN KANGAROO*.

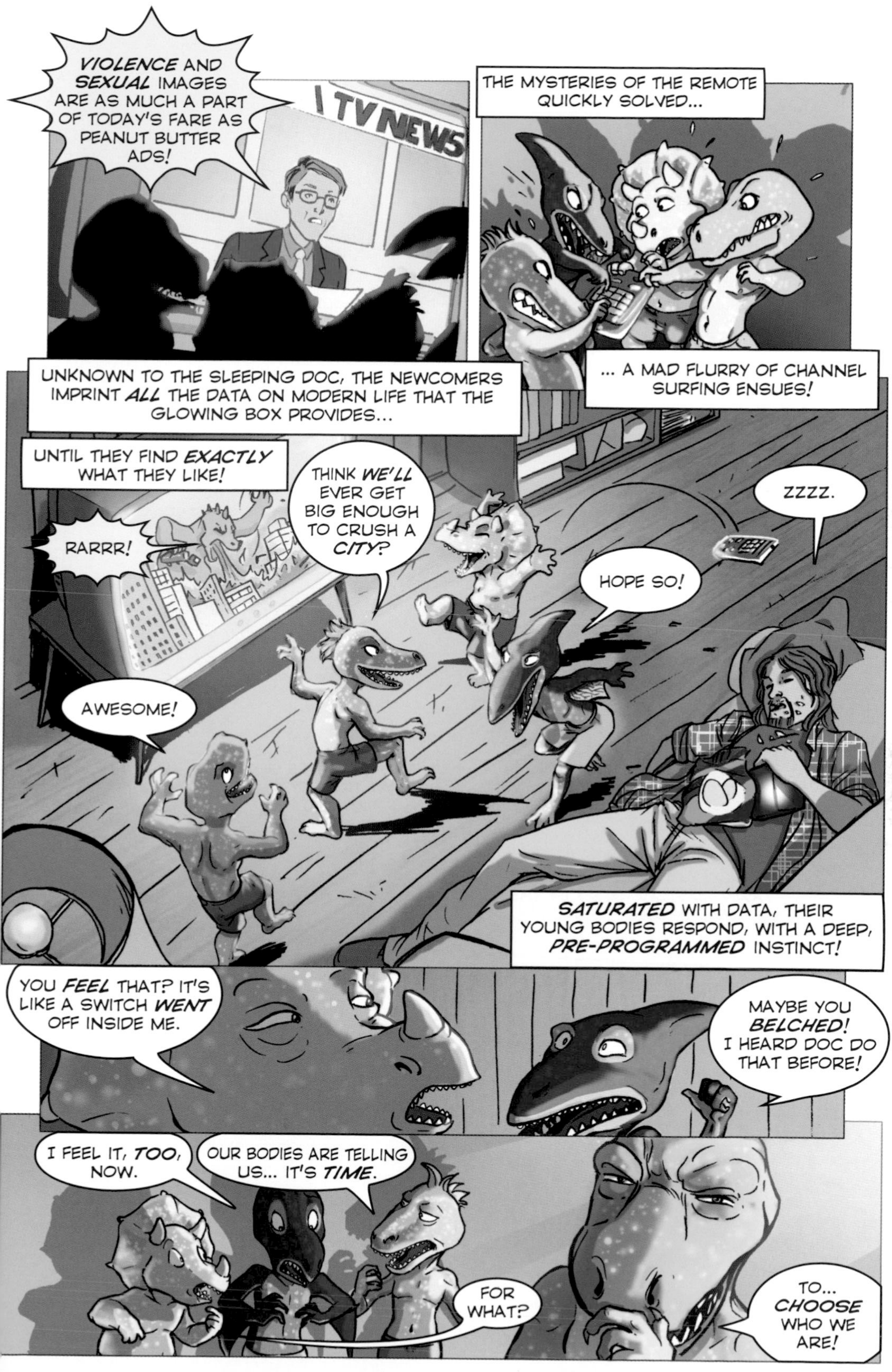
VIOLENCE AND SEXUAL IMAGES ARE AS MUCH A PART OF TODAY'S FARE AS PEANUT BUTTER ADS!
TV NEWS
THE MYSTERIES OF THE REMOTE QUICKLY SOLVED...
... A MAD FLURRY OF CHANNEL SURFING ENSUES!
UNKNOWN TO THE SLEEPING DOC, THE NEWCOMERS IMPRINT ALL THE DATA ON MODERN LIFE THAT THE GLOWING BOX PROVIDES...
UNTIL THEY FIND EXACTLY WHAT THEY LIKE!
RARRR!
THINK WE'LL EVER GET BIG ENOUGH TO CRUSH A CITY?
ZZZZ.
HOPE SO!
AWESOME!
SATURATED WITH DATA, THEIR YOUNG BODIES RESPOND, WITH A DEEP, PRE-PROGRAMMED INSTINCT!
YOU FEEL THAT? IT'S LIKE A SWITCH WENT OFF INSIDE ME.
MAYBE YOU BELCHED! I HEARD DOC DO THAT BEFORE!
I FEEL IT, TOO, NOW.
OUR BODIES ARE TELLING US... IT'S TIME.
FOR WHAT?
TO... CHOOSE WHO WE ARE!

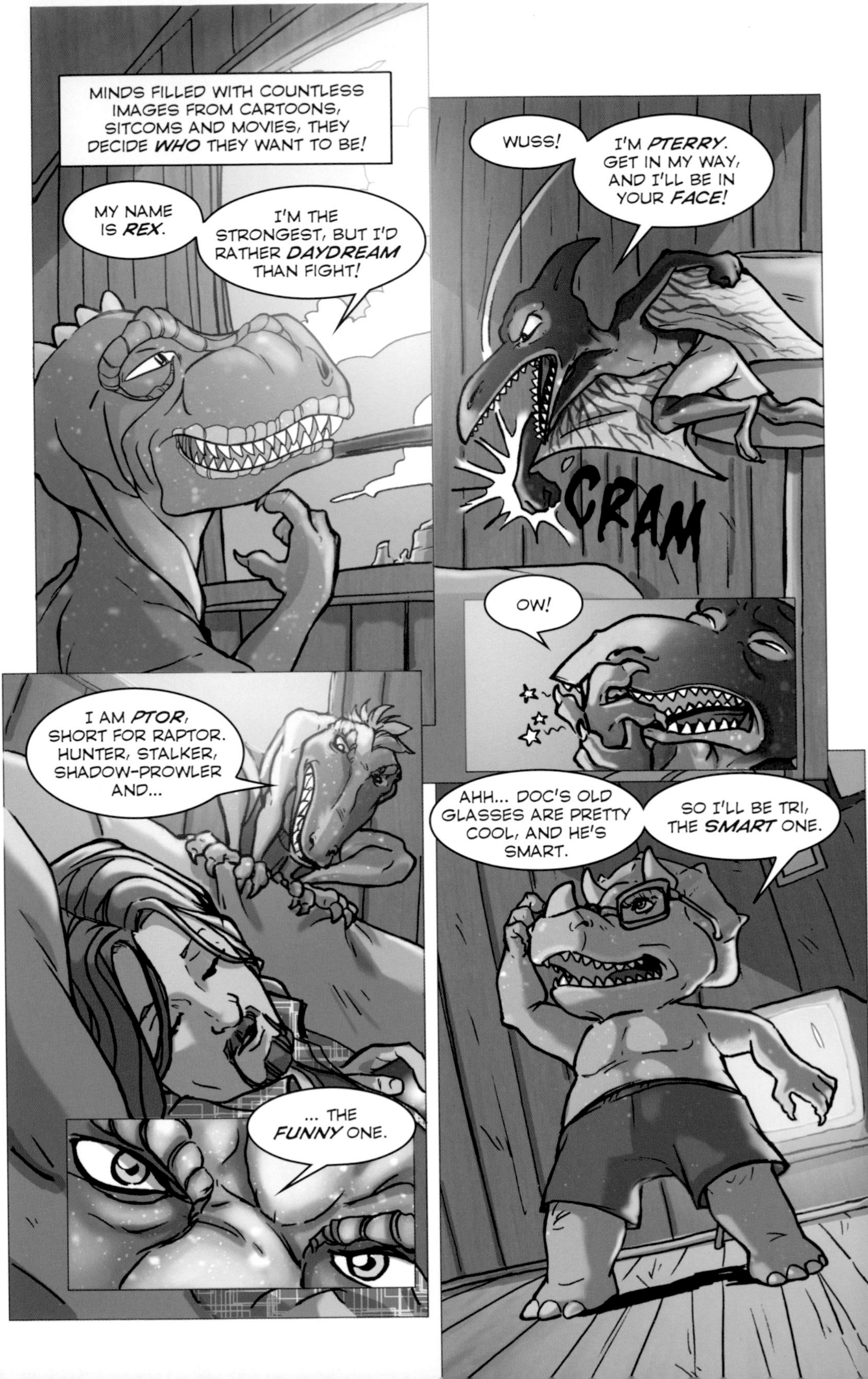
MINDS FILLED WITH COUNTLESS IMAGES FROM CARTOONS, SITCOMS AND MOVIES, THEY DECIDE WHO THEY WANT TO BE!
MY NAME IS REX.
I'M THE STRONGEST, BUT I'D RATHER DAYDREAM THAN FIGHT!
WUSS!
I'M PTERRY. GET IN MY WAY, AND I'LL BE IN YOUR FACE!
CRAM
OW!
I AM PTOR, SHORT FOR RAPTOR. HUNTER, STALKER, SHADOW-PROWLER AND...
... THE FUNNY ONE.
AHH... DOC'S OLD GLASSES ARE PRETTY COOL, AND HE'S SMART.
SO I'LL BE TRI, THE SMART ONE.

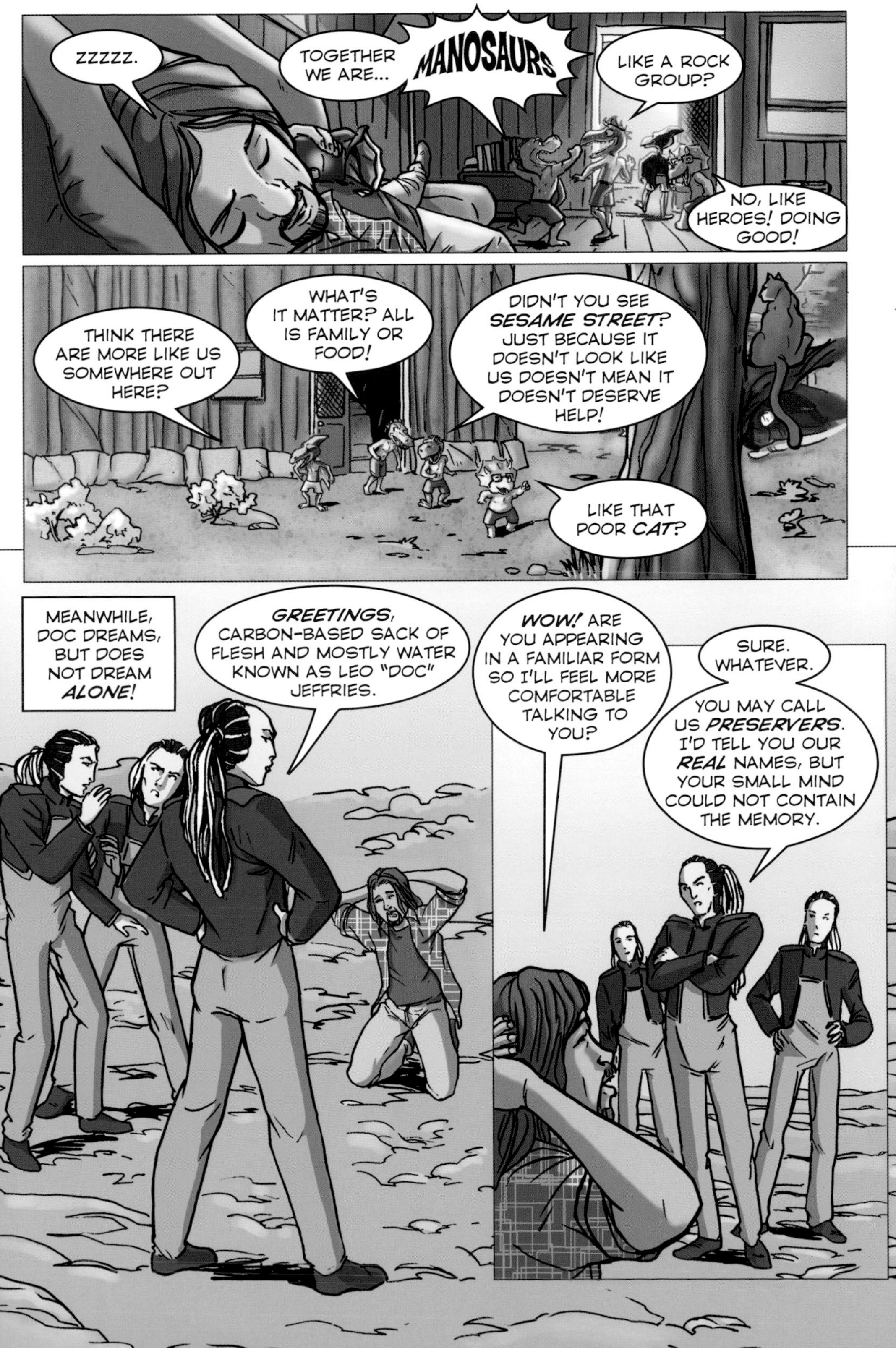
ZZZZZ.
TOGETHER WE ARE...
MANOSAURS
LIKE A ROCK GROUP?
NO, LIKE HEROES! DOING GOOD!
THINK THERE ARE MORE LIKE US SOMEWHERE OUT HERE?
WHAT'S IT MATTER? ALL IS FAMILY OR FOOD!
DIDN'T YOU SEE SESAME STREET? JUST BECAUSE IT DOESN'T LOOK LIKE US DOESN'T MEAN IT DOESN'T DESERVE HELP!
LIKE THAT POOR CAT?
MEANWHILE, DOC DREAMS, BUT DOES NOT DREAM ALONE!
GREETINGS, CARBON-BASED SACK OF FLESH AND MOSTLY WATER KNOWN AS LEO "DOC" JEFFRIES.
WOW! ARE YOU APPEARING IN A FAMILIAR FORM SO I'LL FEEL MORE COMFORTABLE TALKING TO YOU?
SURE. WHATEVER.
YOU MAY CALL US PRESERVERS. I'D TELL YOU OUR REAL NAMES, BUT YOUR SMALL MIND COULD NOT CONTAIN THE MEMORY.

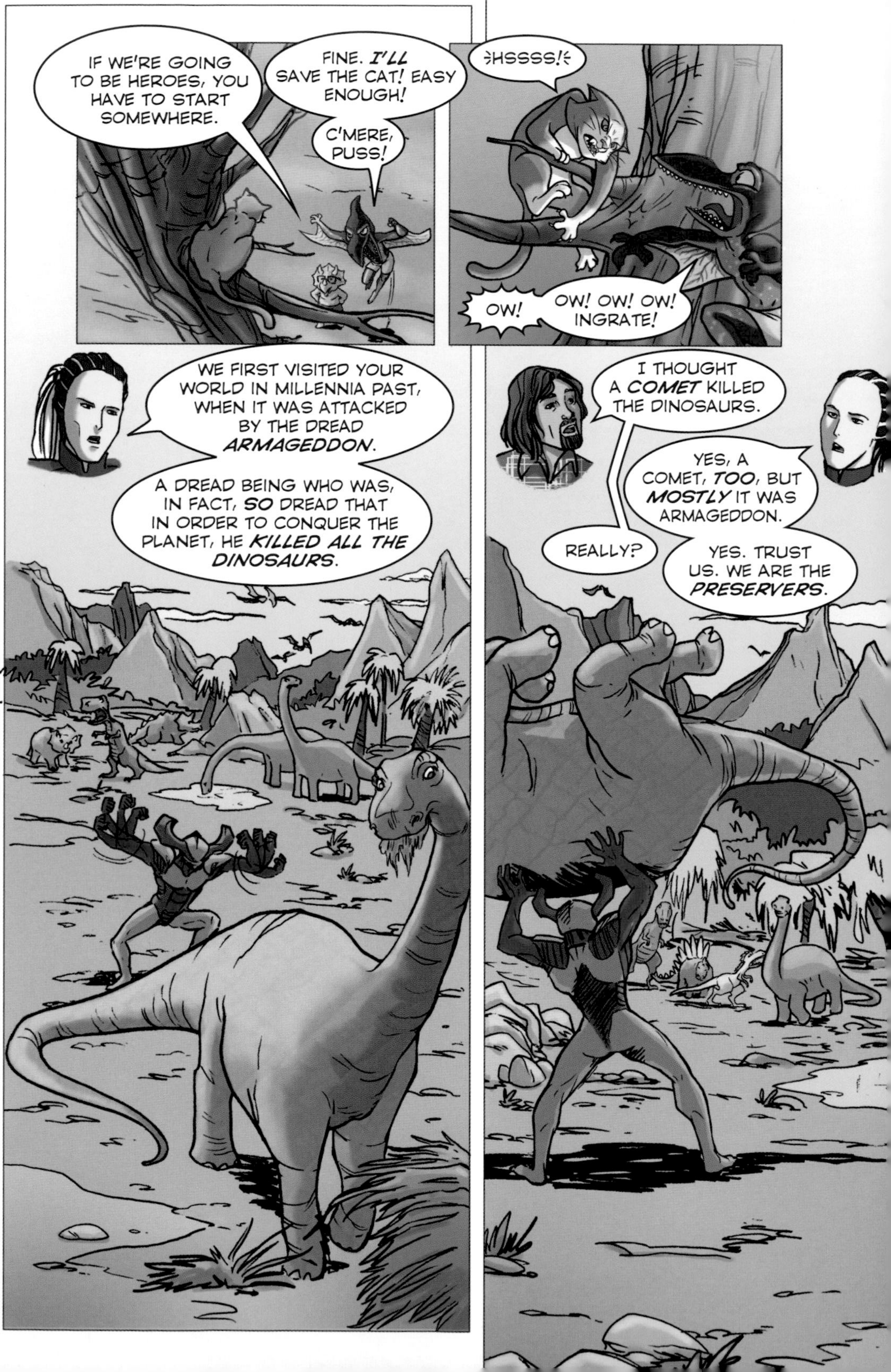
IF WE'RE GOING TO BE HEROES, YOU HAVE TO START SOMEWHERE.
FINE. I'LL SAVE THE CAT! EASY ENOUGH!
C'MERE, PUSS!
HSSSS!
OW!
OW! OW! OW! INGRATE!
WE FIRST VISITED YOUR WORLD IN MILLENNIA PAST, WHEN IT WAS ATTACKED BY THE DREAD ARMAGEDDON.
A DREAD BEING WHO WAS, IN FACT, SO DREAD THAT IN ORDER TO CONQUER THE PLANET, HE KILLED ALL THE DINOSAURS.
I THOUGHT A COMET KILLED THE DINOSAURS.
YES, A COMET, TOO, BUT MOSTLY IT WAS ARMAGEDDON.
REALLY?
YES. TRUST US. WE ARE THE PRESERVERS.

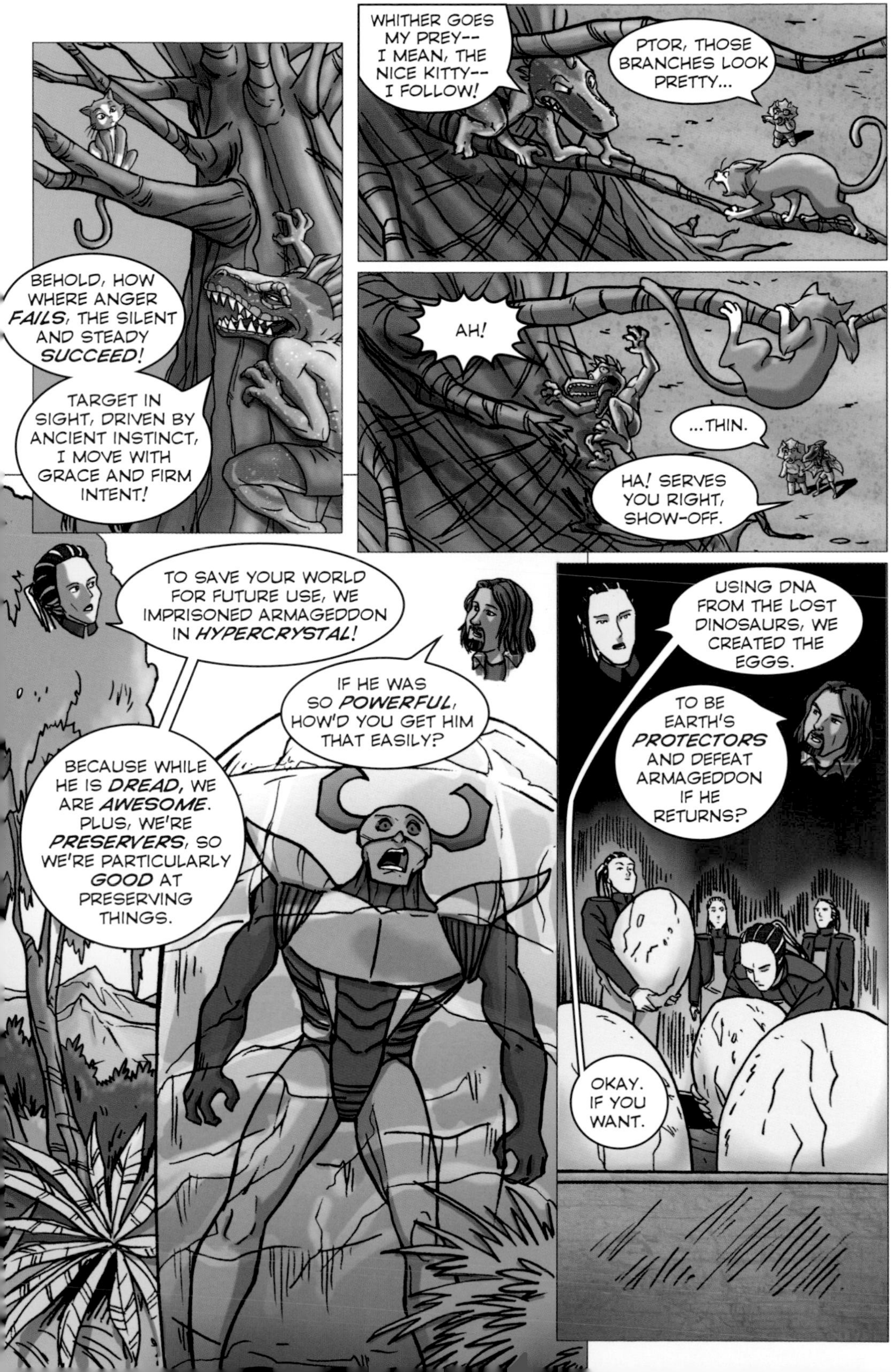
BEHOLD, HOW WHERE ANGER FAILS, THE SILENT AND STEADY SUCCEED!
TARGET IN SIGHT, DRIVEN BY ANCIENT INSTINCT, I MOVE WITH GRACE AND FIRM INTENT!
WHITHER GOES MY PREY-- I MEAN, THE NICE KITTY-- I FOLLOW!
PTOR, THOSE BRANCHES LOOK PRETTY...
AH!
...THIN.
HA! SERVES YOU RIGHT, SHOW-OFF.
TO SAVE YOUR WORLD FOR FUTURE USE, WE IMPRISONED ARMAGEDDON IN HYPERCRYSTAL!
IF HE WAS SO POWERFUL, HOW'D YOU GET HIM THAT EASILY?
BECAUSE WHILE HE IS DREAD, WE ARE AWESOME. PLUS, WE'RE PRESERVERS, SO WE'RE PARTICULARLY GOOD AT PRESERVING THINGS.
USING DNA FROM THE LOST DINOSAURS, WE CREATED THE EGGS.
TO BE EARTH'S PROTECTORS AND DEFEAT ARMAGEDDON IF HE RETURNS?
OKAY. IF YOU WANT.

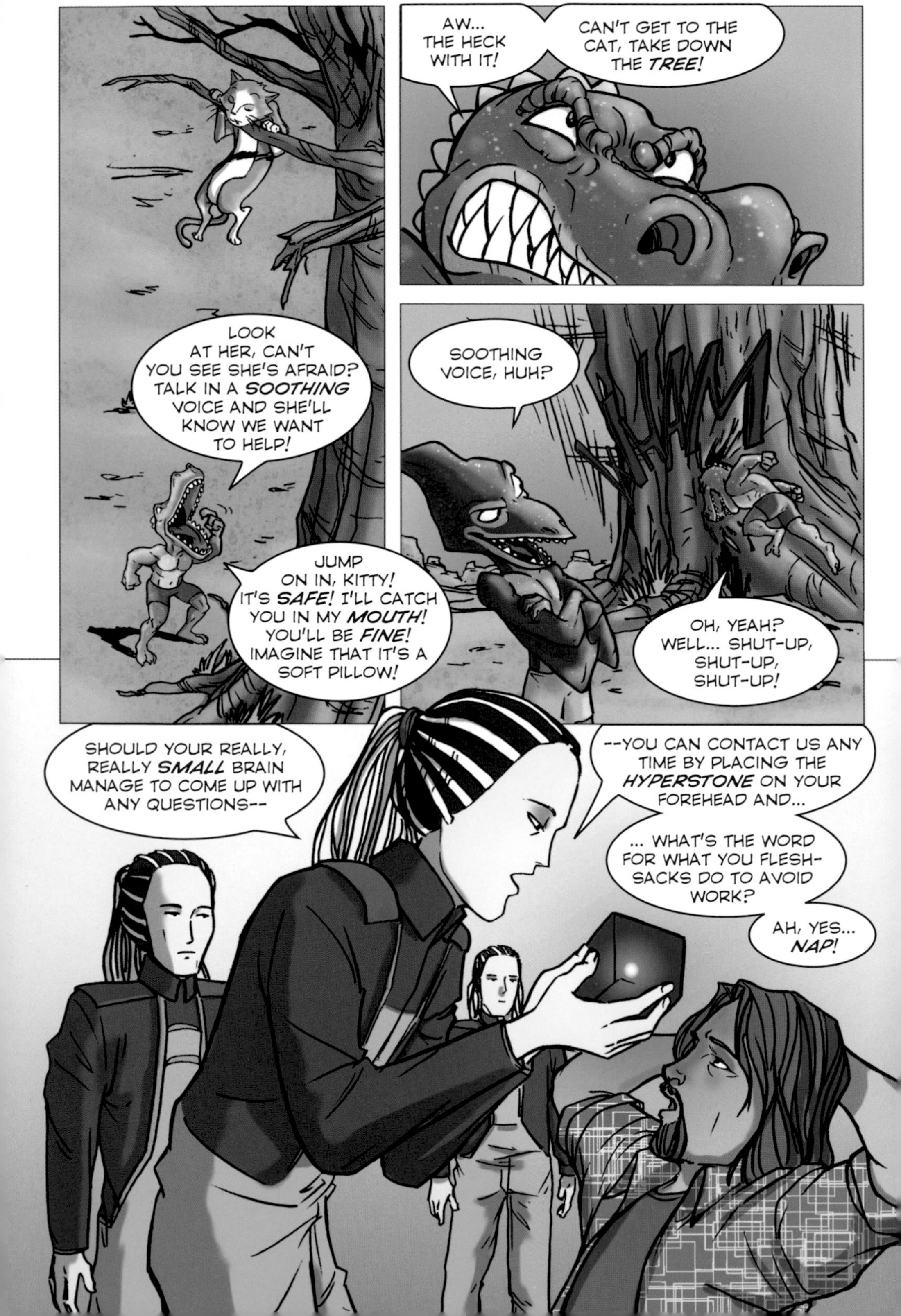
LOOK AT HER, CAN'T YOU SEE SHE'S AFRAID? TALK IN A SOOTHING VOICE AND SHE'LL KNOW WE WANT TO HELP!
JUMP ON IN, KITTY! IT'S SAFE! I'LL CATCH YOU IN MY MOUTH! YOU'LL BE FINE! IMAGINE THAT IT'S A SOFT PILLOW!
AW... THE HECK WITH IT!
CAN'T GET TO THE CAT, TAKE DOWN THE TREE!
SOOTHING VOICE, HUH?
WHAM
OH, YEAH? WELL... SHUT-UP, SHUT-UP, SHUT-UP!
SHOULD YOUR REALLY, REALLY SMALL BRAIN MANAGE TO COME UP WITH ANY QUESTIONS--
--YOU CAN CONTACT US ANY TIME BY PLACING THE HYPERSTONE ON YOUR FOREHEAD AND...
... WHAT'S THE WORD FOR WHAT YOU FLESH-SACKS DO TO AVOID WORK?
AH, YES... NAP!

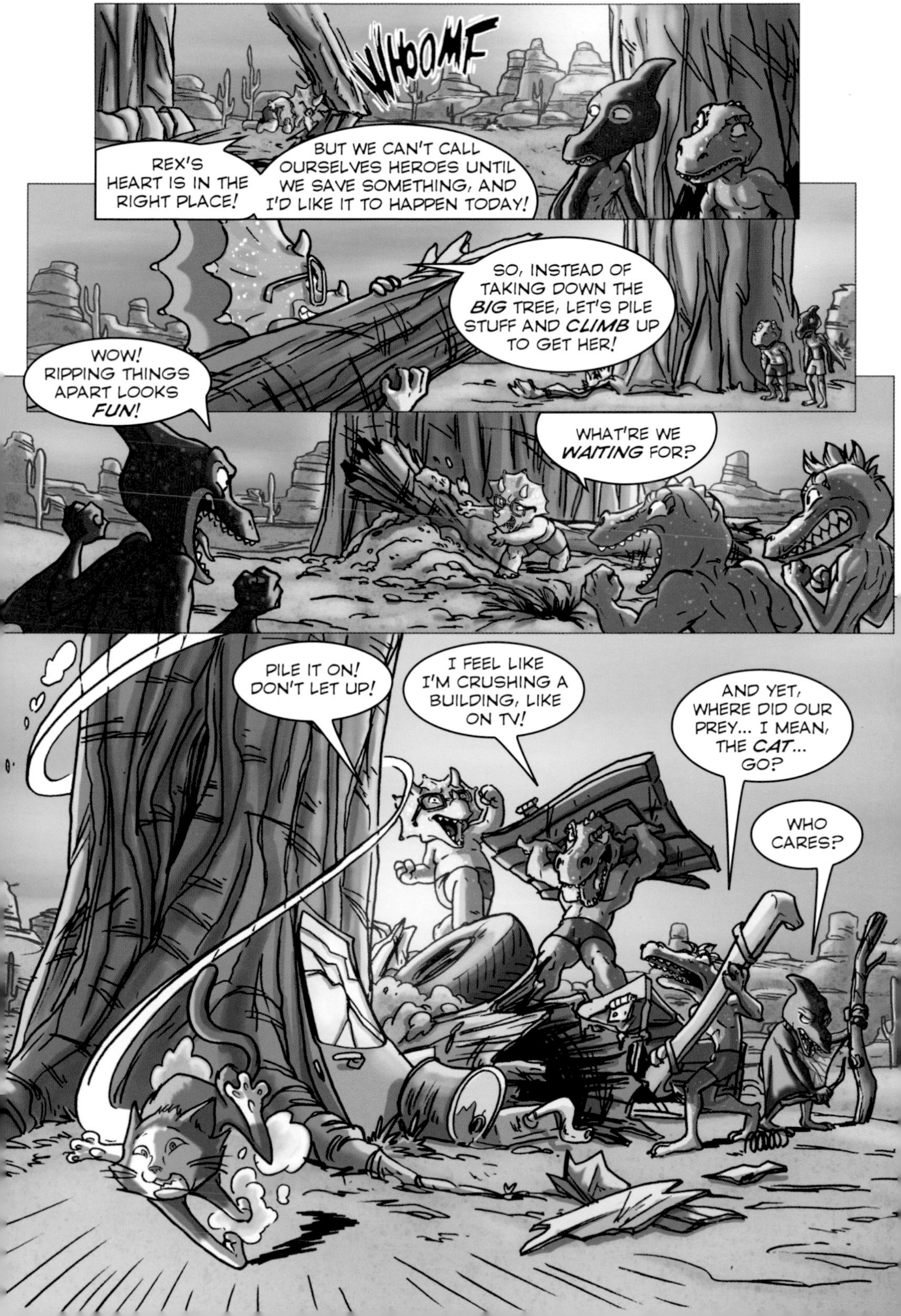
WHOOMF
REX'S HEART IS IN THE RIGHT PLACE!
BUT WE CAN'T CALL OURSELVES HEROES UNTIL WE SAVE SOMETHING, AND I'D LIKE IT TO HAPPEN TODAY!
SO, INSTEAD OF TAKING DOWN THE BIG TREE, LET'S PILE STUFF AND CLIMB UP TO GET HER!
WOW! RIPPING THINGS APART LOOKS FUN!
WHAT'RE WE WAITING FOR?
PILE IT ON! DON'T LET UP!
I FEEL LIKE I'M CRUSHING A BUILDING, LIKE ON TV!
AND YET, WHERE DID OUR PREY... I MEAN, THE CAT... GO?
WHO CARES?

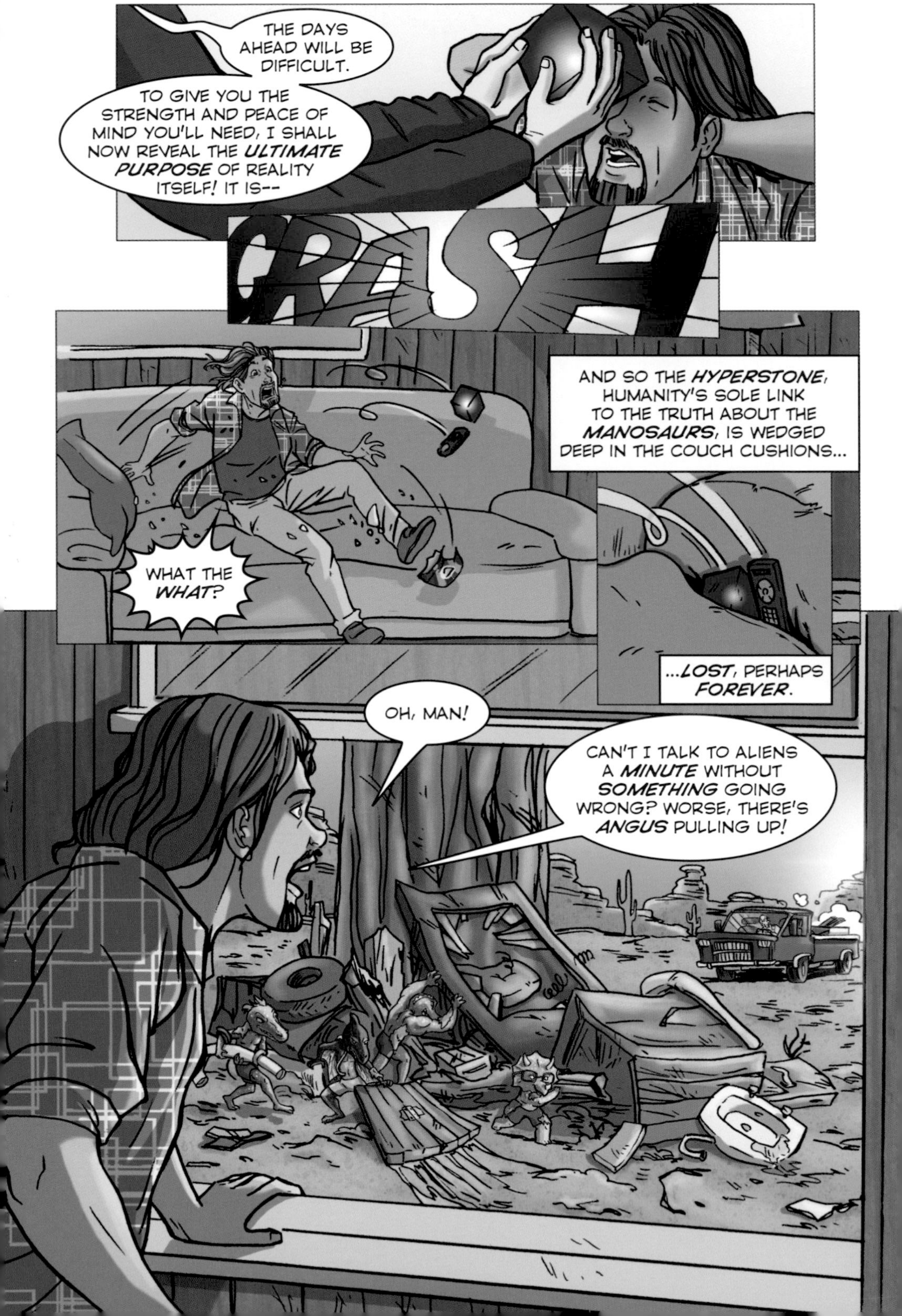
THE DAYS AHEAD WILL BE DIFFICULT.
TO GIVE YOU THE STRENGTH AND PEACE OF MIND YOU'LL NEED, I SHALL NOW REVEAL THE *ULTIMATE PURPOSE* OF REALITY ITSELF! IT IS--
CRASH
AND SO THE *HYPERSTONE*, HUMANITY'S SOLE LINK TO THE TRUTH ABOUT THE *MANOSAURS*, IS WEDGED DEEP IN THE COUCH CUSHIONS...
WHAT THE *WHAT*?
...*LOST*, PERHAPS *FOREVER*.
OH, MAN!
CAN'T I TALK TO ALIENS A *MINUTE* WITHOUT *SOMETHING* GOING WRONG? WORSE, THERE'S *ANGUS* PULLING UP!

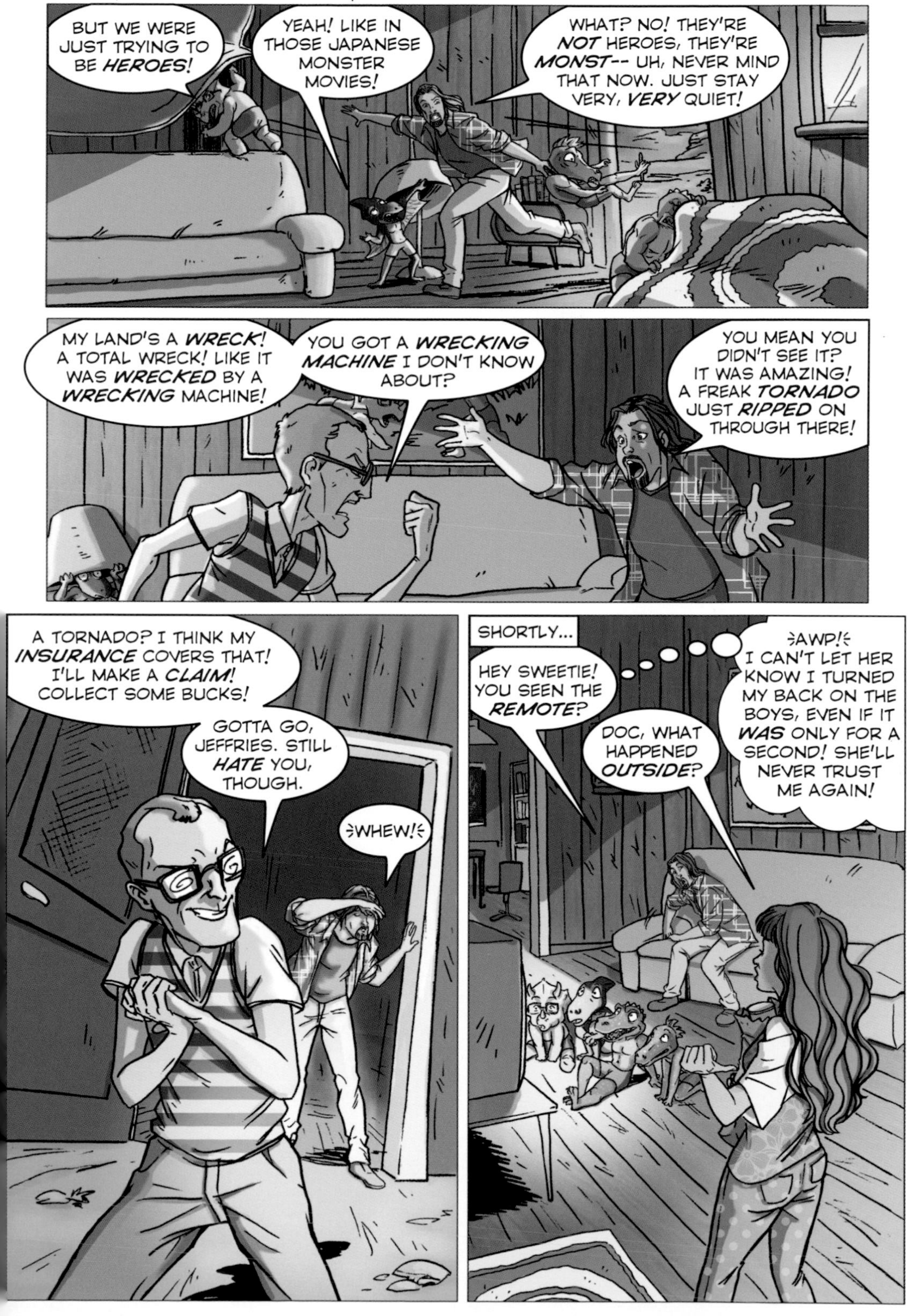

BUT WE WERE JUST TRYING TO BE HEROES!
YEAH! LIKE IN THOSE JAPANESE MONSTER MOVIES!
WHAT? NO! THEY'RE NOT HEROES, THEY'RE MONST-- UH, NEVER MIND THAT NOW. JUST STAY VERY, VERY QUIET!
MY LAND'S A WRECK! A TOTAL WRECK! LIKE IT WAS WRECKED BY A WRECKING MACHINE!
YOU GOT A WRECKING MACHINE I DON'T KNOW ABOUT?
YOU MEAN YOU DIDN'T SEE IT? IT WAS AMAZING! A FREAK TORNADO JUST RIPPED ON THROUGH THERE!
A TORNADO? I THINK MY INSURANCE COVERS THAT! I'LL MAKE A CLAIM! COLLECT SOME BUCKS!
GOTTA GO, JEFFRIES. STILL HATE YOU, THOUGH.
WHEW!
SHORTLY...
HEY SWEETIE! YOU SEEN THE REMOTE?
DOC, WHAT HAPPENED OUTSIDE?
AWP! I CAN'T LET HER KNOW I TURNED MY BACK ON THE BOYS, EVEN IF IT WAS ONLY FOR A SECOND! SHE'LL NEVER TRUST ME AGAIN!

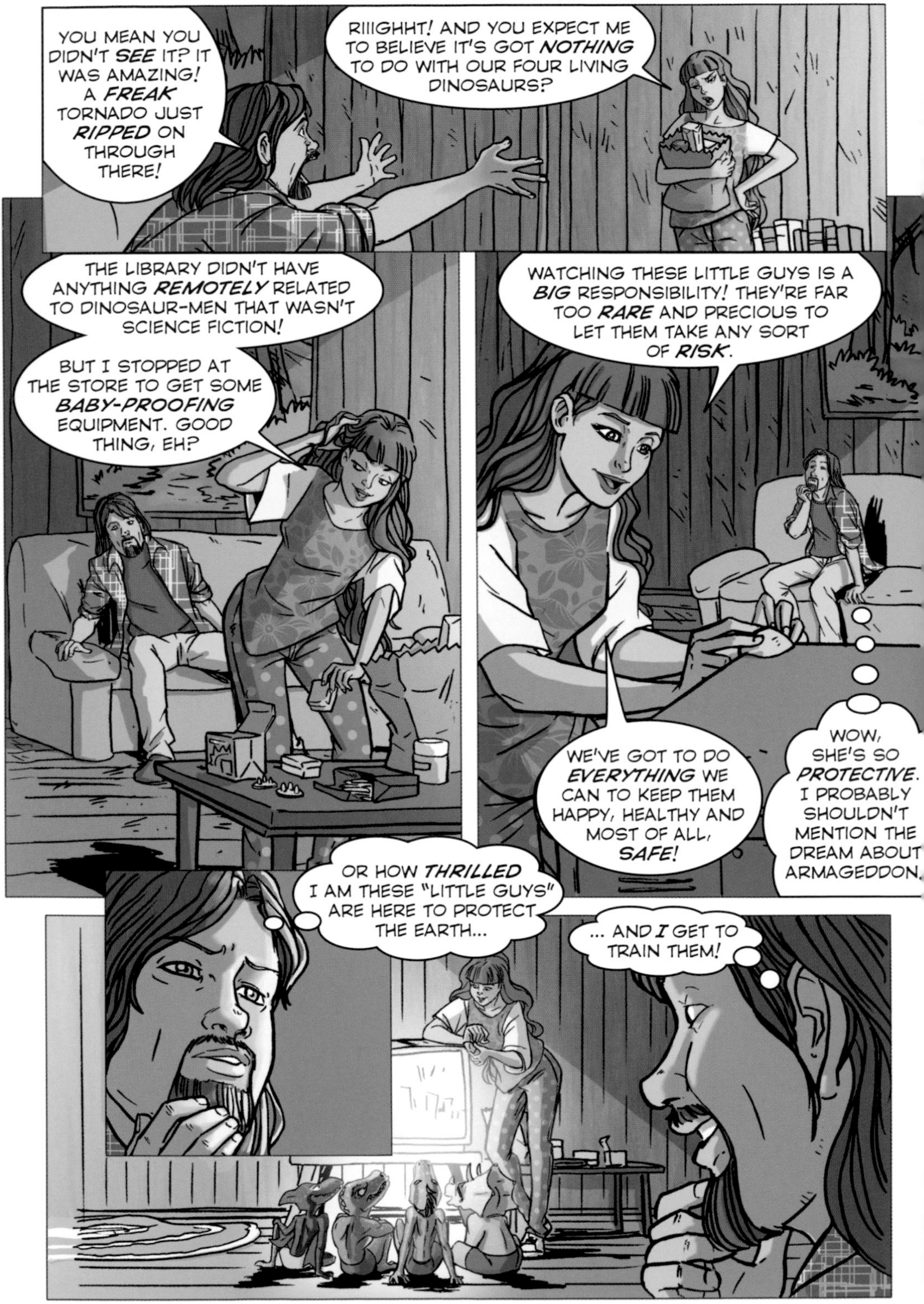
YOU MEAN YOU DIDN'T SEE IT? IT WAS AMAZING! A FREAK TORNADO JUST RIPPED ON THROUGH THERE!
RIIIGHHT! AND YOU EXPECT ME TO BELIEVE IT'S GOT NOTHING TO DO WITH OUR FOUR LIVING DINOSAURS?
THE LIBRARY DIDN'T HAVE ANYTHING REMOTELY RELATED TO DINOSAUR-MEN THAT WASN'T SCIENCE FICTION!
BUT I STOPPED AT THE STORE TO GET SOME BABY-PROOFING EQUIPMENT. GOOD THING, EH?
WATCHING THESE LITTLE GUYS IS A BIG RESPONSIBILITY! THEY'RE FAR TOO RARE AND PRECIOUS TO LET THEM TAKE ANY SORT OF RISK.
WE'VE GOT TO DO EVERYTHING WE CAN TO KEEP THEM HAPPY, HEALTHY AND MOST OF ALL, SAFE!
WOW, SHE'S SO PROTECTIVE. I PROBABLY SHOULDN'T MENTION THE DREAM ABOUT ARMAGEDDON.
OR HOW THRILLED I AM THESE "LITTLE GUYS" ARE HERE TO PROTECT THE EARTH...
... AND I GET TO TRAIN THEM!

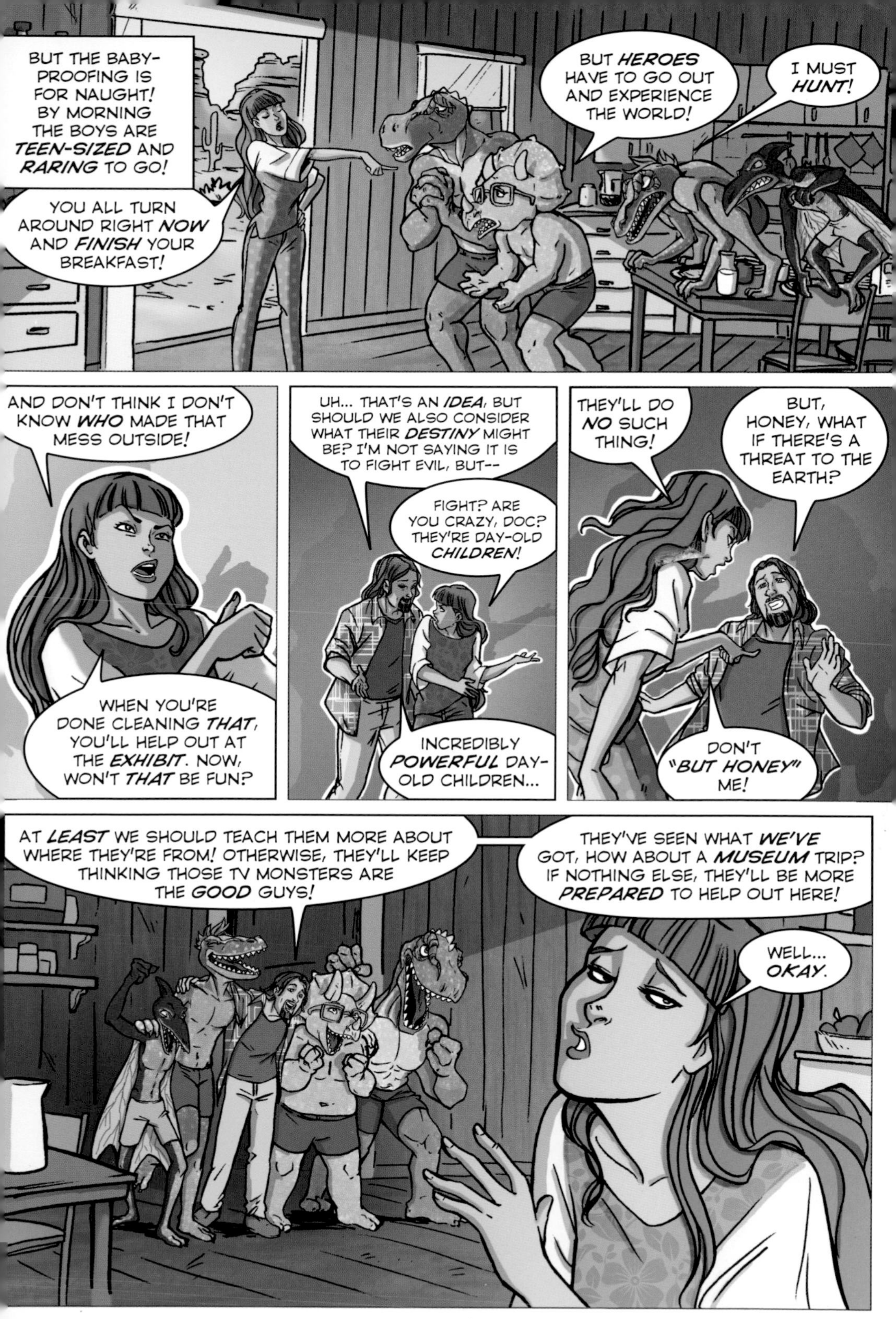
BUT THE BABY-PROOFING IS FOR NAUGHT! BY MORNING THE BOYS ARE TEEN-SIZED AND RARING TO GO!
YOU ALL TURN AROUND RIGHT NOW AND FINISH YOUR BREAKFAST!
BUT HEROES HAVE TO GO OUT AND EXPERIENCE THE WORLD!
I MUST HUNT!
AND DON'T THINK I DON'T KNOW WHO MADE THAT MESS OUTSIDE!
WHEN YOU'RE DONE CLEANING THAT, YOU'LL HELP OUT AT THE EXHIBIT. NOW, WON'T THAT BE FUN?
UH... THAT'S AN IDEA, BUT SHOULD WE ALSO CONSIDER WHAT THEIR DESTINY MIGHT BE? I'M NOT SAYING IT IS TO FIGHT EVIL, BUT--
FIGHT? ARE YOU CRAZY, DOC? THEY'RE DAY-OLD CHILDREN!
INCREDIBLY POWERFUL DAY-OLD CHILDREN...
THEY'LL DO NO SUCH THING!
BUT, HONEY, WHAT IF THERE'S A THREAT TO THE EARTH?
DON'T "BUT HONEY" ME!
AT LEAST WE SHOULD TEACH THEM MORE ABOUT WHERE THEY'RE FROM! OTHERWISE, THEY'LL KEEP THINKING THOSE TV MONSTERS ARE THE GOOD GUYS!
THEY'VE SEEN WHAT WE'VE GOT, HOW ABOUT A MUSEUM TRIP? IF NOTHING ELSE, THEY'LL BE MORE PREPARED TO HELP OUT HERE!
WELL... OKAY.

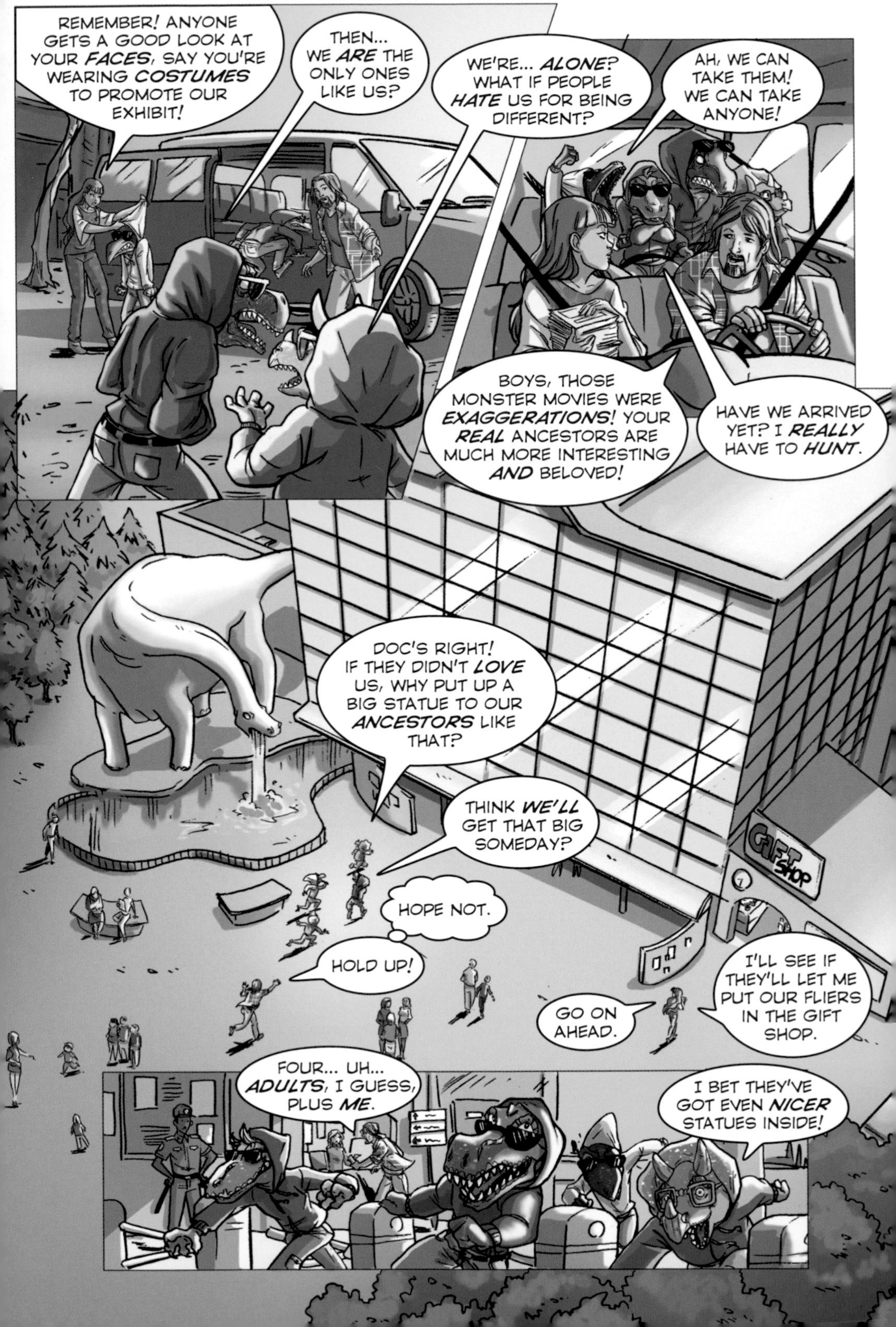
REMEMBER! ANYONE GETS A GOOD LOOK AT YOUR FACES, SAY YOU'RE WEARING COSTUMES TO PROMOTE OUR EXHIBIT!
THEN... WE ARE THE ONLY ONES LIKE US?
WE'RE... ALONE? WHAT IF PEOPLE HATE US FOR BEING DIFFERENT?
AH, WE CAN TAKE THEM! WE CAN TAKE ANYONE!
BOYS, THOSE MONSTER MOVIES WERE EXAGGERATIONS! YOUR REAL ANCESTORS ARE MUCH MORE INTERESTING AND BELOVED!
HAVE WE ARRIVED YET? I REALLY HAVE TO HUNT.
DOC'S RIGHT! IF THEY DIDN'T LOVE US, WHY PUT UP A BIG STATUE TO OUR ANCESTORS LIKE THAT?
THINK WE'LL GET THAT BIG SOMEDAY?
HOPE NOT.
GIFT SHOP
HOLD UP!
GO ON AHEAD.
I'LL SEE IF THEY'LL LET ME PUT OUR FLIERS IN THE GIFT SHOP.
FOUR... UH... ADULTS, I GUESS, PLUS ME.
I BET THEY'VE GOT EVEN NICER STATUES INSIDE!

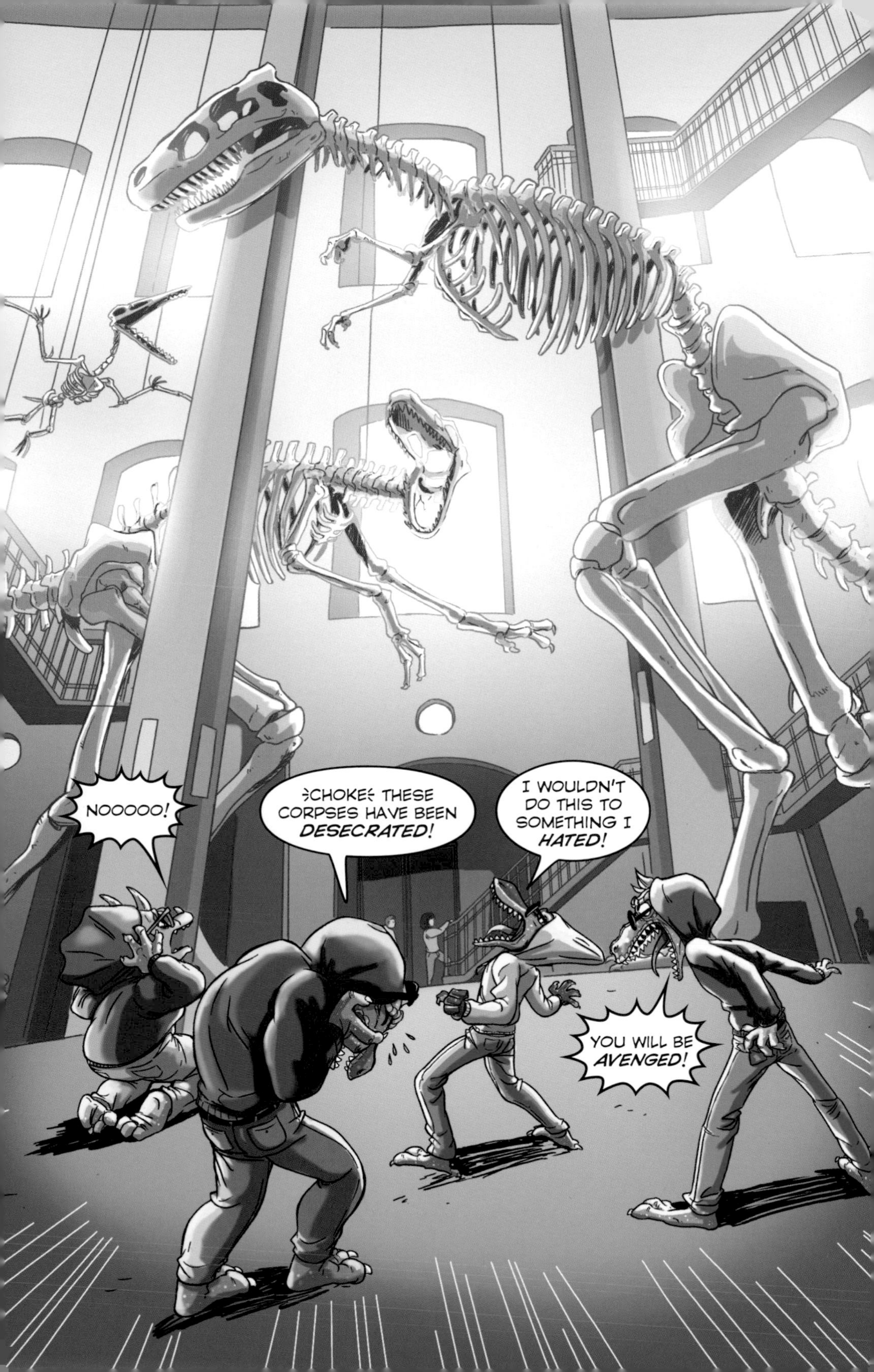
NOOOOO!
⊰CHOKE⊱ THESE CORPSES HAVE BEEN DESECRATED!
I WOULDN'T DO THIS TO SOMETHING I HATED!
YOU WILL BE AVENGED!

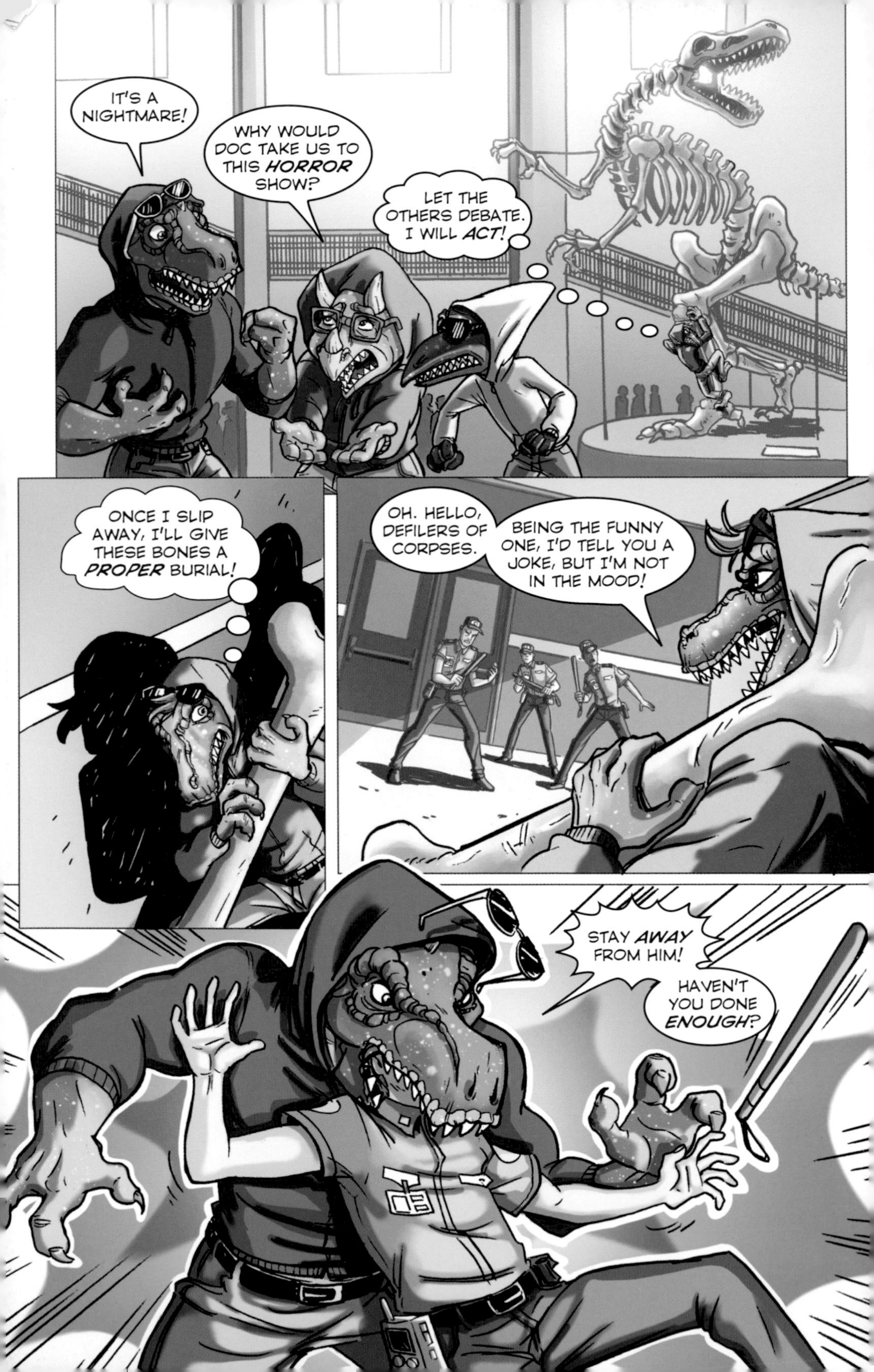
IT'S A NIGHTMARE!
WHY WOULD DOC TAKE US TO THIS *HORROR* SHOW?
LET THE OTHERS DEBATE. I WILL *ACT*!
ONCE I SLIP AWAY, I'LL GIVE THESE BONES A *PROPER* BURIAL!
OH. HELLO, DEFILERS OF CORPSES.
BEING THE FUNNY ONE, I'D TELL YOU A JOKE, BUT I'M NOT IN THE MOOD!
STAY *AWAY* FROM HIM!
HAVEN'T YOU DONE *ENOUGH*?

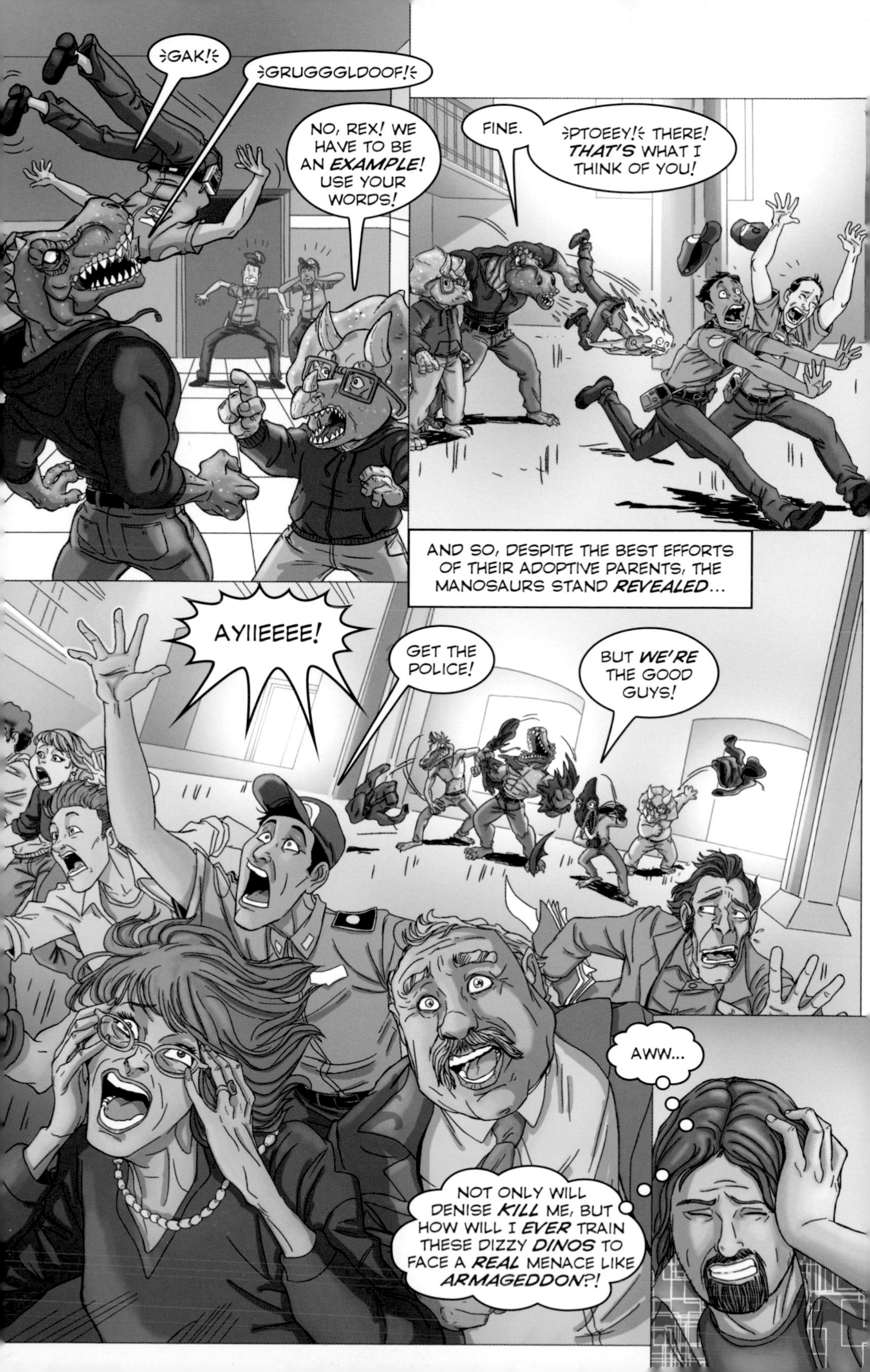
GAK!
GRUGGGLDOOF!
NO, REX! WE HAVE TO BE AN EXAMPLE! USE YOUR WORDS!
FINE.
PTOEEY! THERE! THAT'S WHAT I THINK OF YOU!
AND SO, DESPITE THE BEST EFFORTS OF THEIR ADOPTIVE PARENTS, THE MANOSAURS STAND REVEALED...
AYIIEEEE!
GET THE POLICE!
BUT WE'RE THE GOOD GUYS!
AWW...
NOT ONLY WILL DENISE KILL ME, BUT HOW WILL I EVER TRAIN THESE DIZZY DINOS TO FACE A REAL MENACE LIKE ARMAGEDDON?!

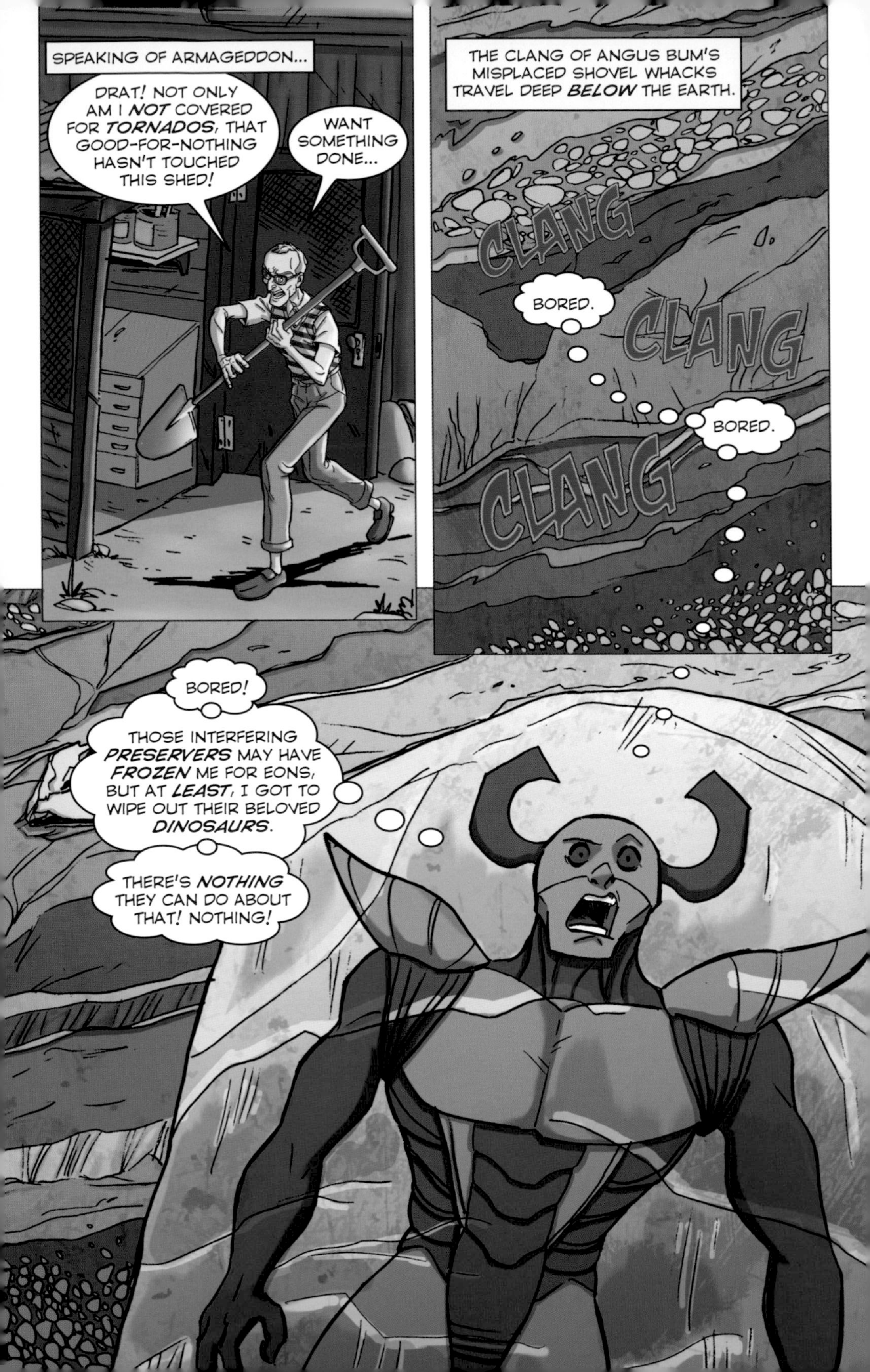
SPEAKING OF ARMAGEDDON...
DRAT! NOT ONLY AM I NOT COVERED FOR TORNADOS, THAT GOOD-FOR-NOTHING HASN'T TOUCHED THIS SHED!
WANT SOMETHING DONE...
THE CLANG OF ANGUS BUM'S MISPLACED SHOVEL WHACKS TRAVEL DEEP BELOW THE EARTH.
CLANG
BORED.
CLANG
BORED.
CLANG
BORED!
THOSE INTERFERING PRESERVERS MAY HAVE FROZEN ME FOR EONS, BUT AT LEAST, I GOT TO WIPE OUT THEIR BELOVED DINOSAURS.
THERE'S NOTHING THEY CAN DO ABOUT THAT! NOTHING!

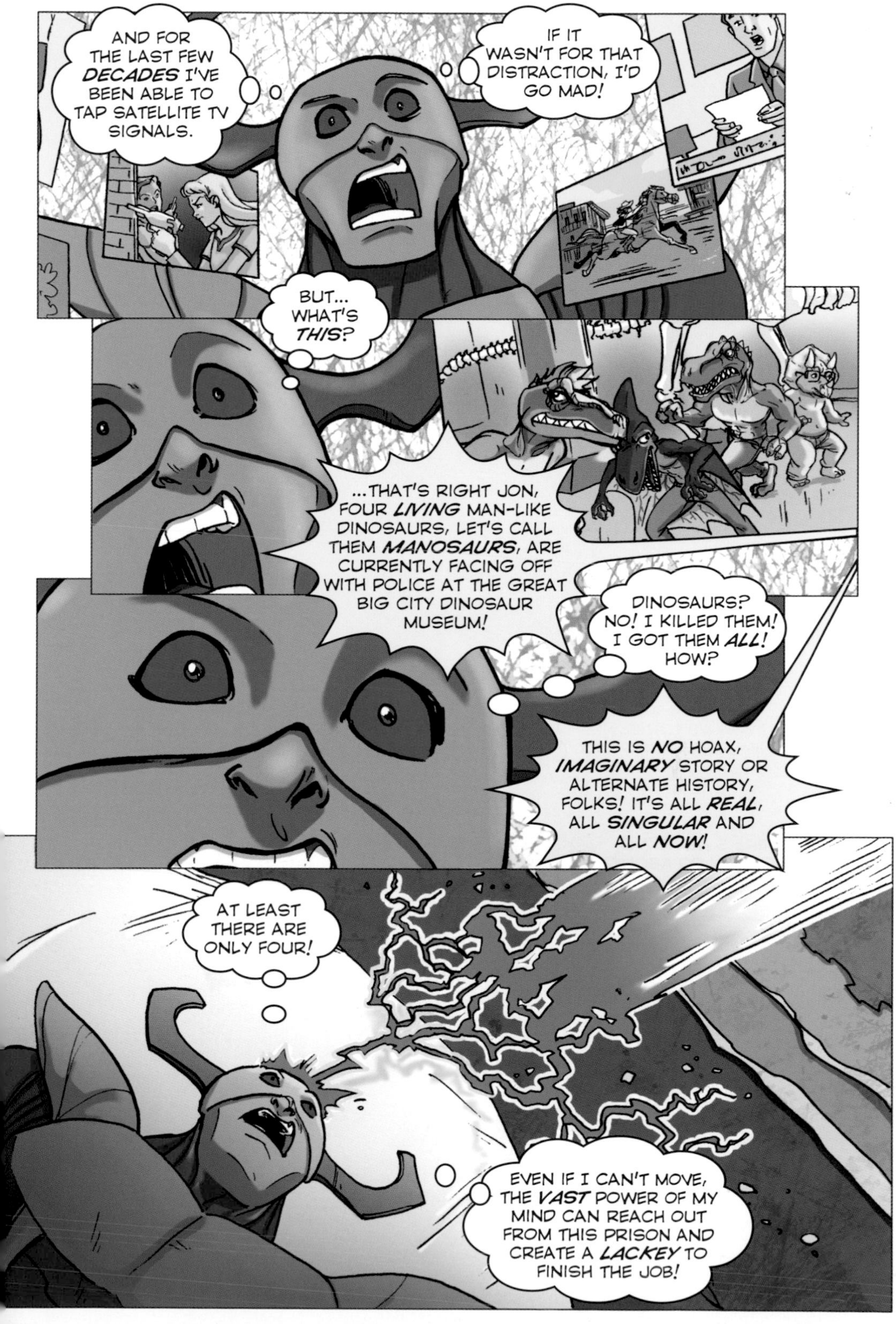
AND FOR THE LAST FEW DECADES I'VE BEEN ABLE TO TAP SATELLITE TV SIGNALS.
IF IT WASN'T FOR THAT DISTRACTION, I'D GO MAD!
BUT... WHAT'S THIS?
...THAT'S RIGHT JON, FOUR LIVING MAN-LIKE DINOSAURS, LET'S CALL THEM MANOSAURS, ARE CURRENTLY FACING OFF WITH POLICE AT THE GREAT BIG CITY DINOSAUR MUSEUM!
DINOSAURS? NO! I KILLED THEM! I GOT THEM ALL! HOW?
THIS IS NO HOAX, IMAGINARY STORY OR ALTERNATE HISTORY, FOLKS! IT'S ALL REAL, ALL SINGULAR AND ALL NOW!
AT LEAST THERE ARE ONLY FOUR!
EVEN IF I CAN'T MOVE, THE VAST POWER OF MY MIND CAN REACH OUT FROM THIS PRISON AND CREATE A LACKEY TO FINISH THE JOB!

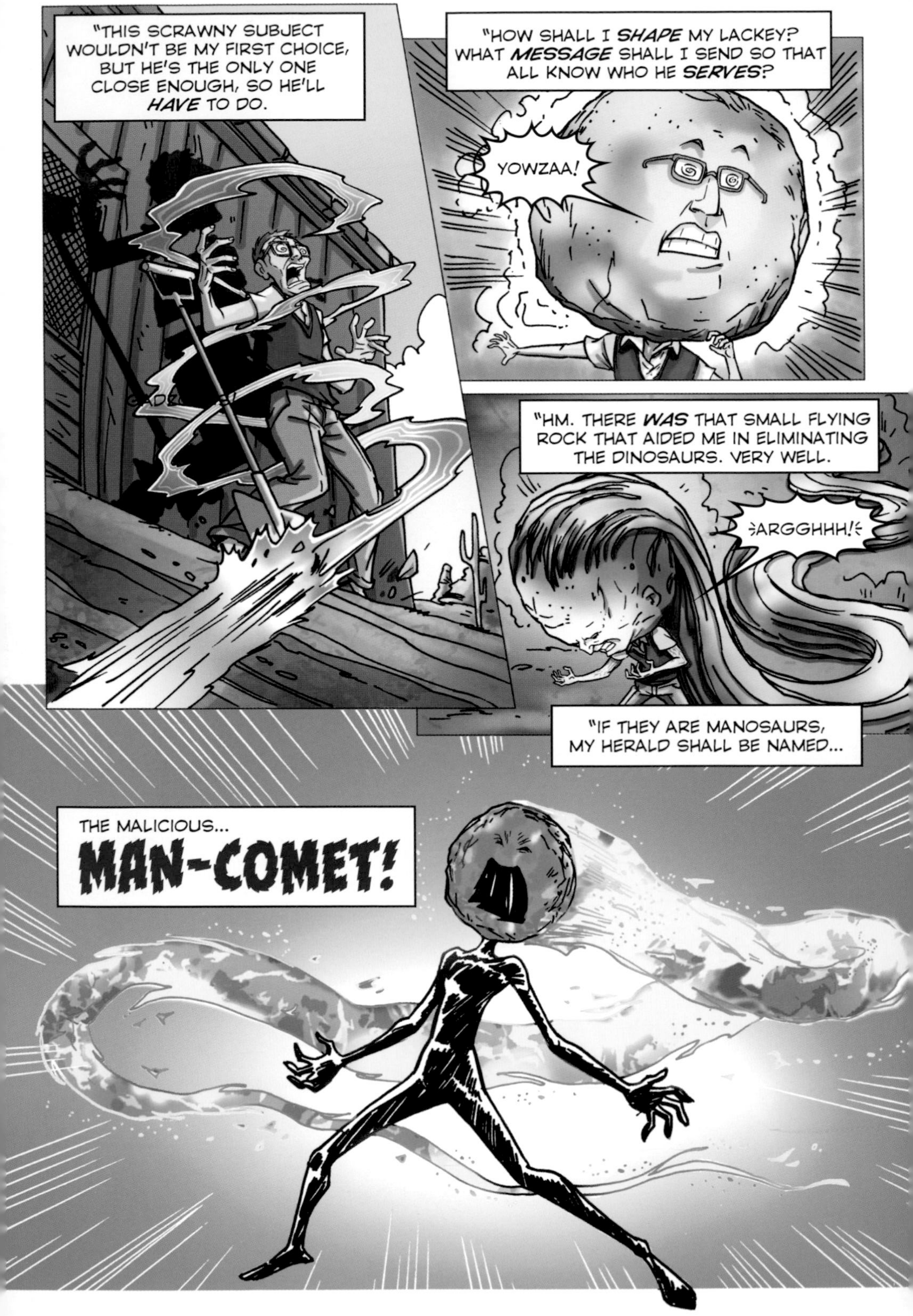
"THIS SCRAWNY SUBJECT WOULDN'T BE MY FIRST CHOICE, BUT HE'S THE ONLY ONE CLOSE ENOUGH, SO HE'LL *HAVE* TO DO.
"HOW SHALL I *SHAPE* MY LACKEY? WHAT *MESSAGE* SHALL I SEND SO THAT ALL KNOW WHO HE *SERVES*?
YOWZAA!
"HM. THERE *WAS* THAT SMALL FLYING ROCK THAT AIDED ME IN ELIMINATING THE DINOSAURS. VERY WELL.
ARGGHHH!
"IF THEY ARE MANOSAURS, MY HERALD SHALL BE NAMED...
THE MALICIOUS...
MAN-COMET!

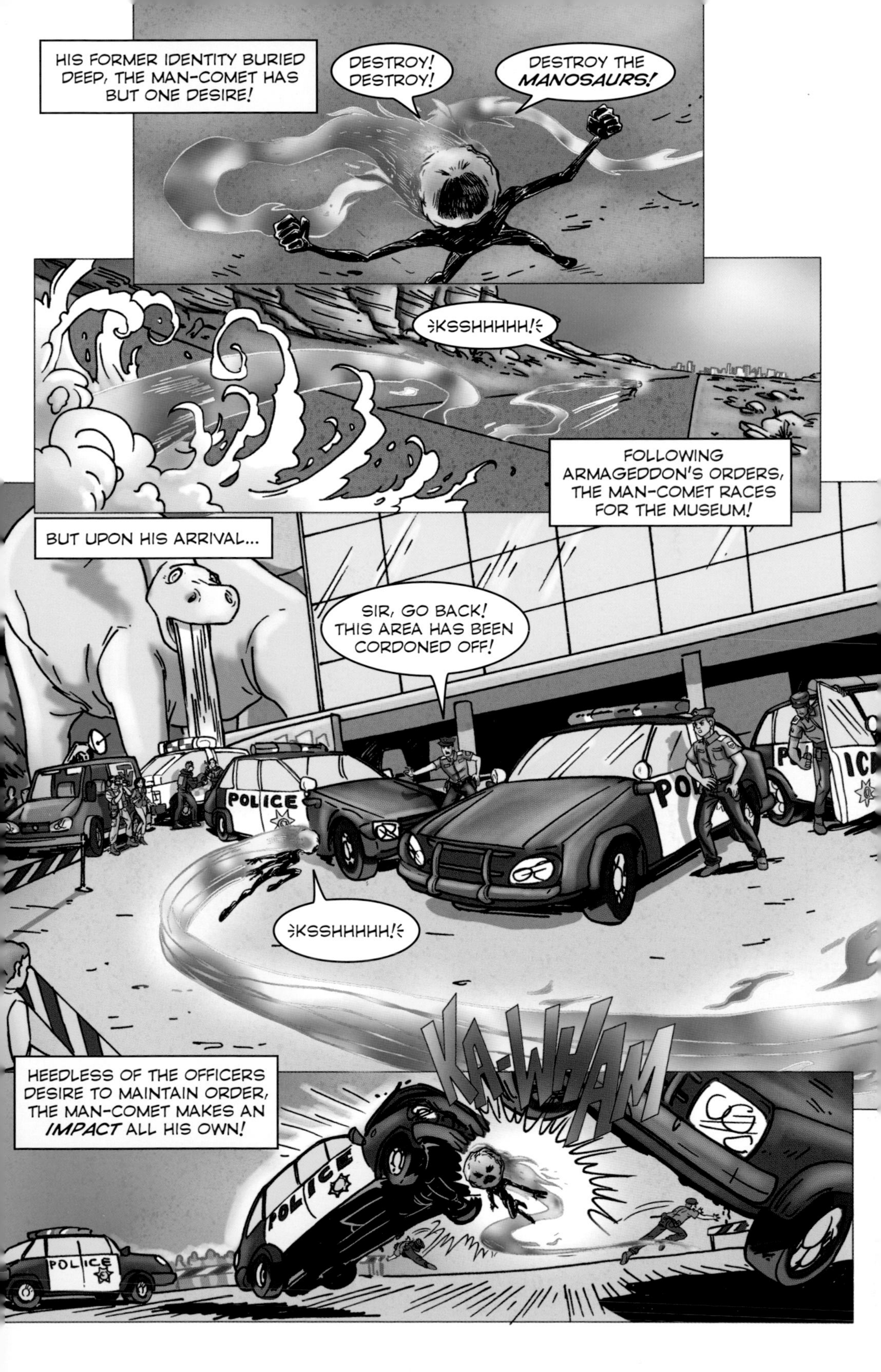
HIS FORMER IDENTITY BURIED DEEP, THE MAN-COMET HAS BUT ONE DESIRE!
DESTROY! DESTROY!
DESTROY THE *MANOSAURS!*
KSSHHHHH!
FOLLOWING ARMAGEDDON'S ORDERS, THE MAN-COMET RACES FOR THE MUSEUM!
BUT UPON HIS ARRIVAL...
SIR, GO BACK! THIS AREA HAS BEEN CORDONED OFF!
POLICE
KSSHHHHH!
KA-WHAM
HEEDLESS OF THE OFFICERS DESIRE TO MAINTAIN ORDER, THE MAN-COMET MAKES AN *IMPACT* ALL HIS OWN!
POLICE
POLICE

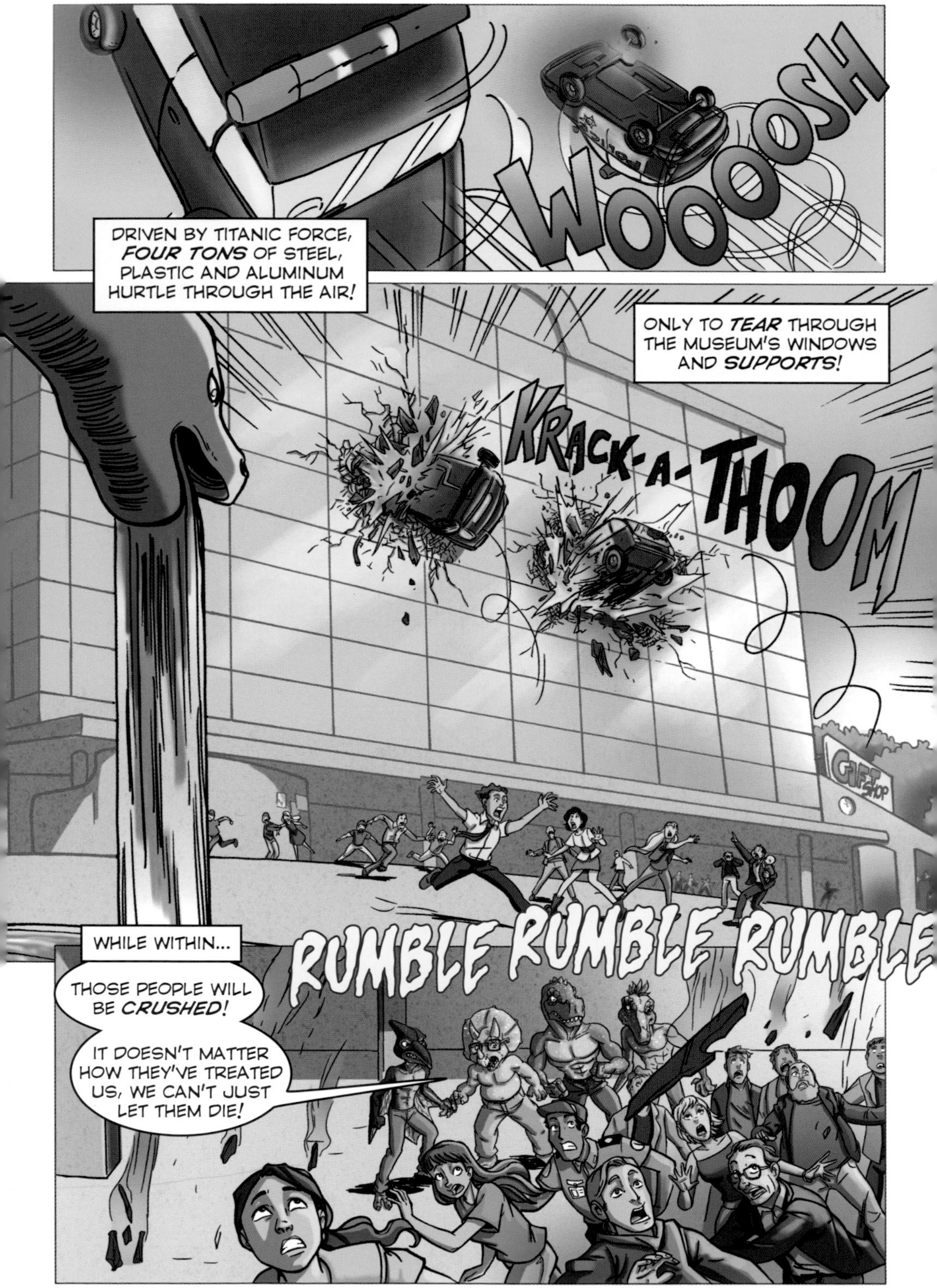
WOOOOSH
DRIVEN BY TITANIC FORCE, FOUR TONS OF STEEL, PLASTIC AND ALUMINUM HURTLE THROUGH THE AIR!
ONLY TO TEAR THROUGH THE MUSEUM'S WINDOWS AND SUPPORTS!
KRACK-A-THOOM
GIFT SHOP
RUMBLE RUMBLE RUMBLE
WHILE WITHIN...
THOSE PEOPLE WILL BE CRUSHED!
IT DOESN'T MATTER HOW THEY'VE TREATED US, WE CAN'T JUST LET THEM DIE!

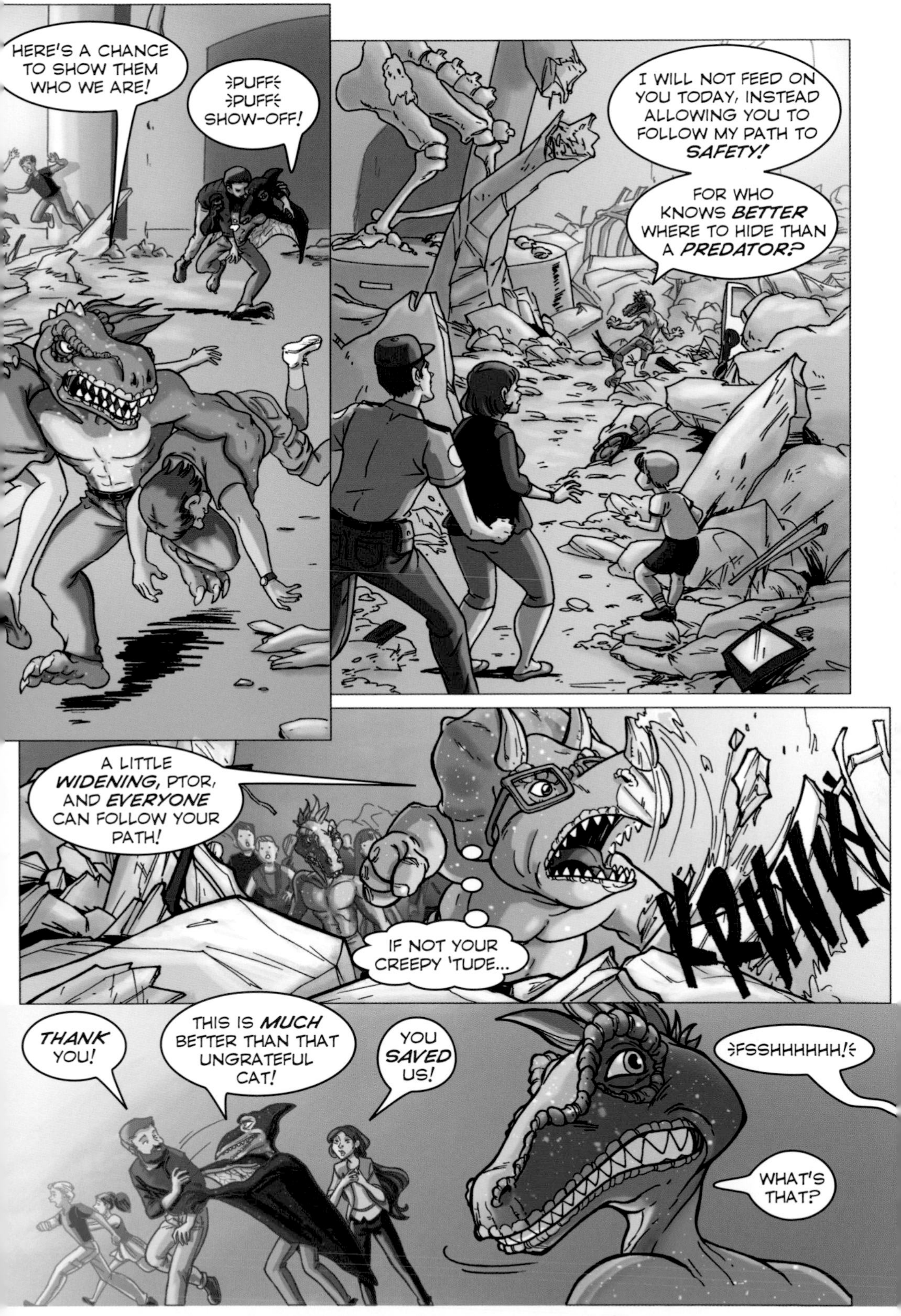
HERE'S A CHANCE TO SHOW THEM WHO WE ARE!
PUFF PUFF SHOW-OFF!
I WILL NOT FEED ON YOU TODAY, INSTEAD ALLOWING YOU TO FOLLOW MY PATH TO SAFETY!
FOR WHO KNOWS BETTER WHERE TO HIDE THAN A PREDATOR?
A LITTLE WIDENING, PTOR, AND EVERYONE CAN FOLLOW YOUR PATH!
IF NOT YOUR CREEPY 'TUDE...
KRUNK
THANK YOU!
THIS IS MUCH BETTER THAN THAT UNGRATEFUL CAT!
YOU SAVED US!
FSSHHHHHH!
WHAT'S THAT?

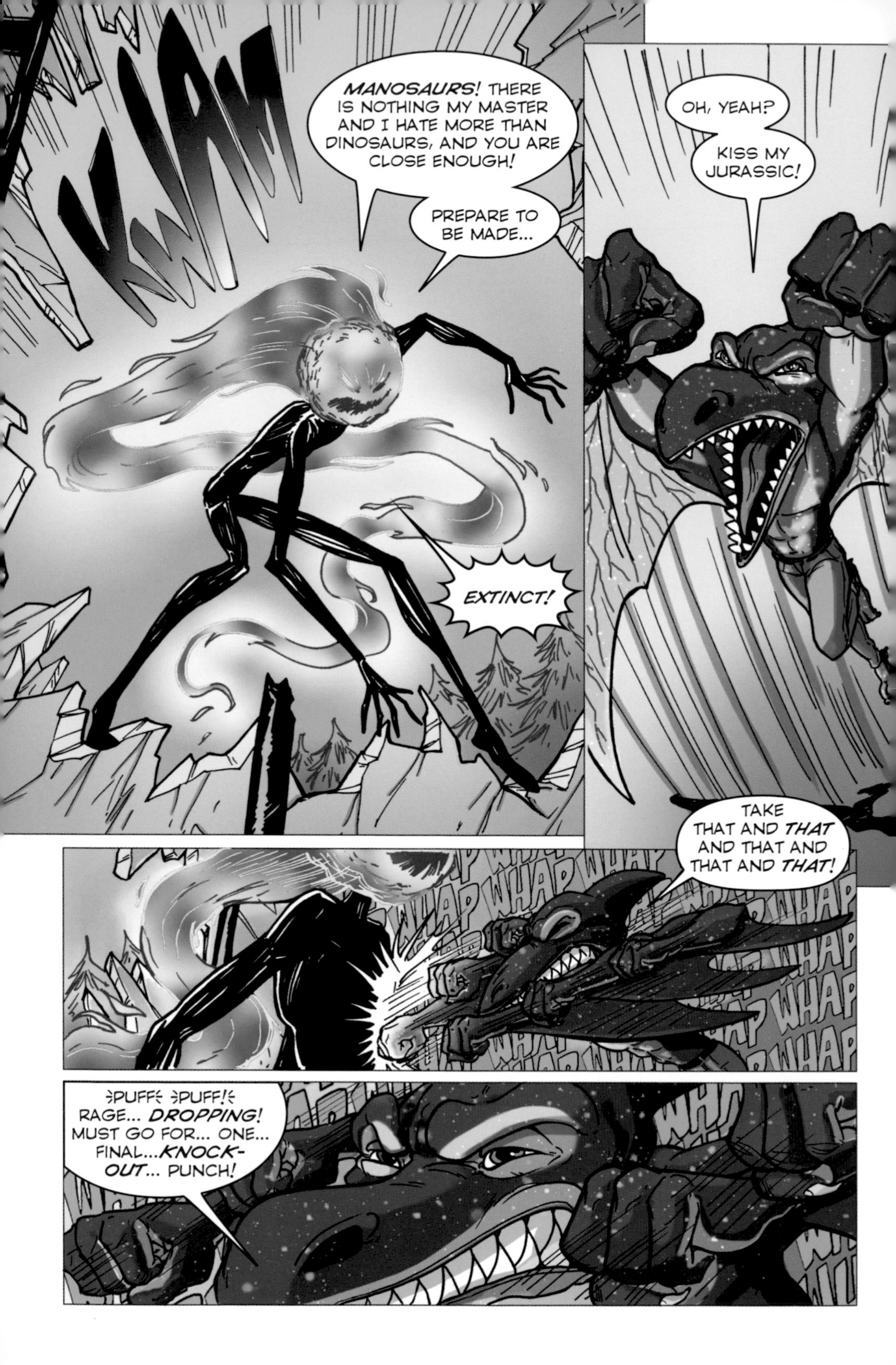
KWAM
MANOSAURS! THERE IS NOTHING MY MASTER AND I HATE MORE THAN DINOSAURS, AND YOU ARE CLOSE ENOUGH!
PREPARE TO BE MADE...
EXTINCT!
OH, YEAH?
KISS MY JURASSIC!
TAKE THAT AND THAT AND THAT AND THAT AND THAT!
WHAP WHAP WHAP WHAP
PUFF PUFF! RAGE... DROPPING! MUST GO FOR... ONE... FINAL...KNOCK-OUT... PUNCH!

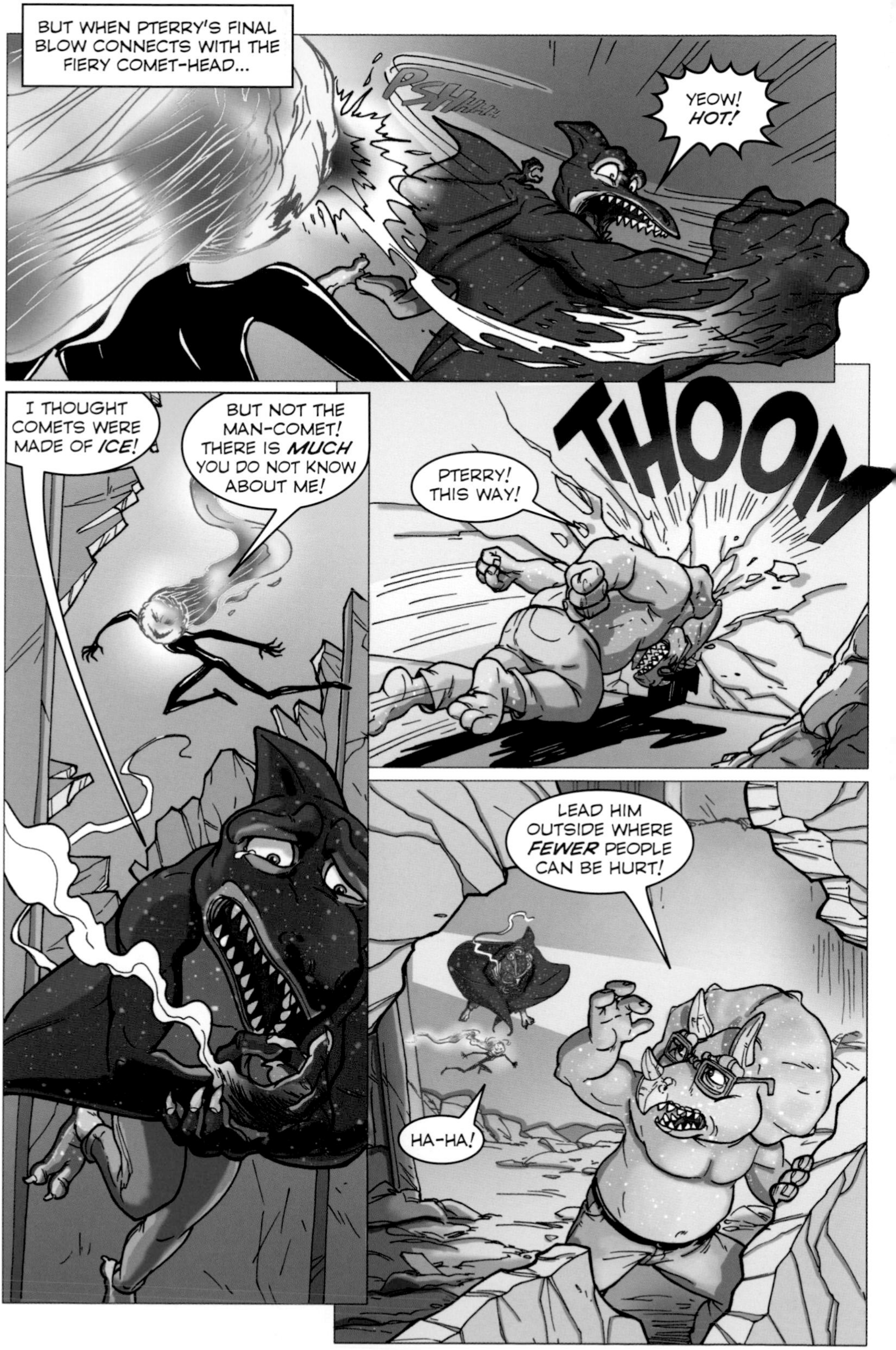
BUT WHEN PTERRY'S FINAL BLOW CONNECTS WITH THE FIERY COMET-HEAD...
PSHHHH
YEOW! HOT!
I THOUGHT COMETS WERE MADE OF ICE!
BUT NOT THE MAN-COMET! THERE IS MUCH YOU DO NOT KNOW ABOUT ME!
THOOM
PTERRY! THIS WAY!
LEAD HIM OUTSIDE WHERE FEWER PEOPLE CAN BE HURT!
HA-HA!

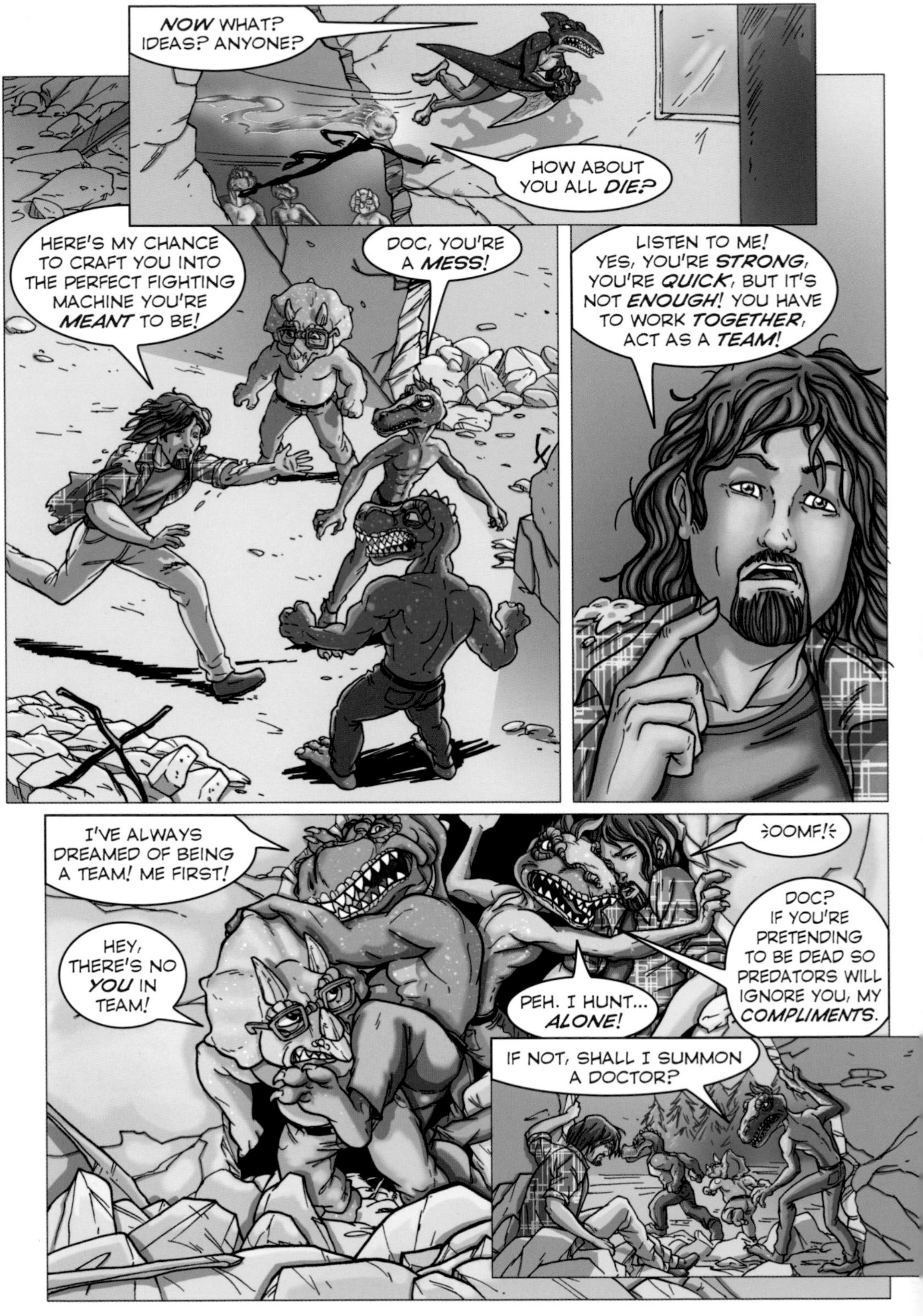
NOW WHAT? IDEAS? ANYONE?
HOW ABOUT YOU ALL DIE?
HERE'S MY CHANCE TO CRAFT YOU INTO THE PERFECT FIGHTING MACHINE YOU'RE MEANT TO BE!
DOC, YOU'RE A MESS!
LISTEN TO ME! YES, YOU'RE STRONG, YOU'RE QUICK, BUT IT'S NOT ENOUGH! YOU HAVE TO WORK TOGETHER, ACT AS A TEAM!
I'VE ALWAYS DREAMED OF BEING A TEAM! ME FIRST!
OOMF!
HEY, THERE'S NO YOU IN TEAM!
PEH. I HUNT... ALONE!
DOC? IF YOU'RE PRETENDING TO BE DEAD SO PREDATORS WILL IGNORE YOU, MY COMPLIMENTS.
IF NOT, SHALL I SUMMON A DOCTOR?

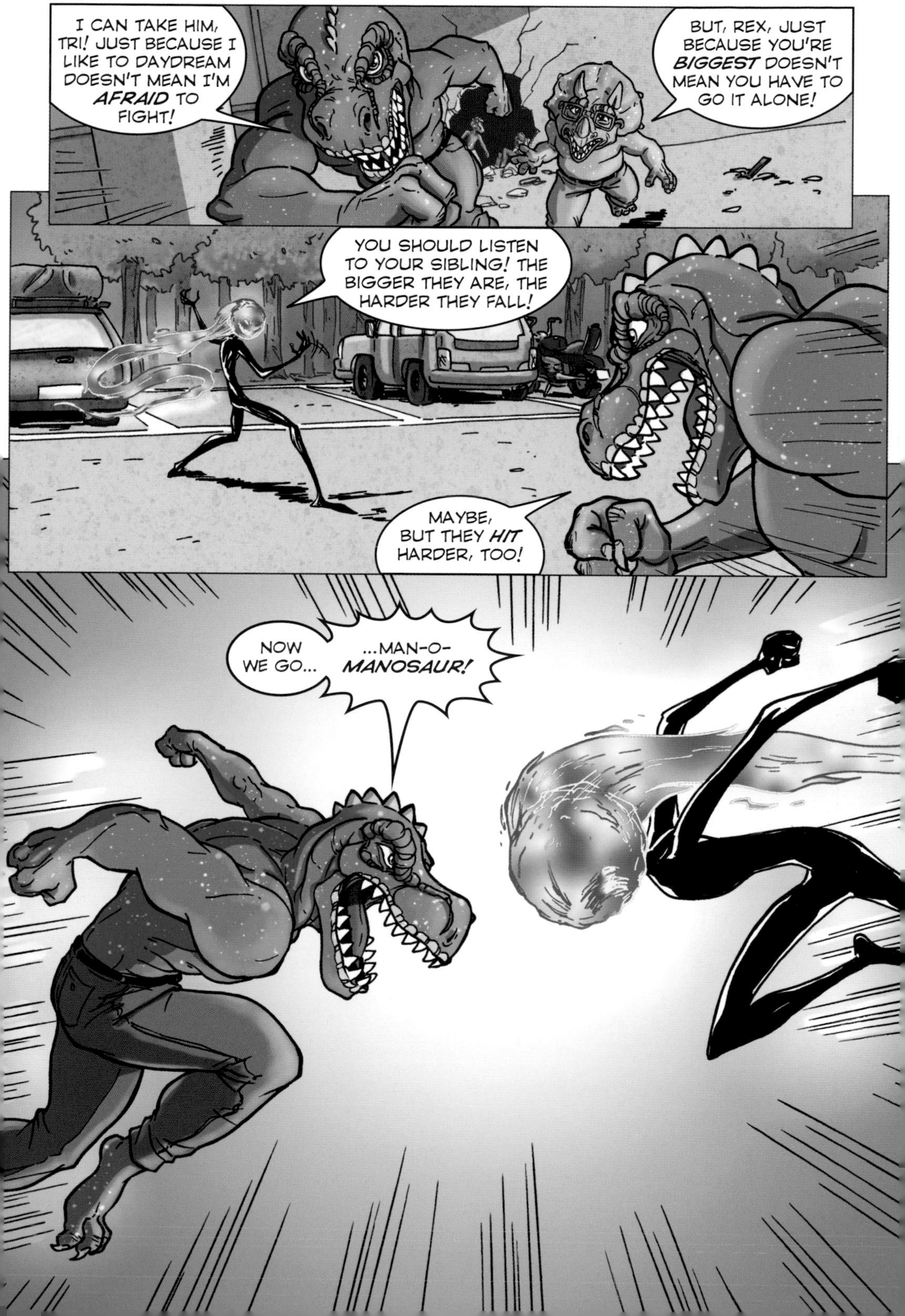
I CAN TAKE HIM, TRI! JUST BECAUSE I LIKE TO DAYDREAM DOESN'T MEAN I'M *AFRAID* TO FIGHT!
BUT, REX, JUST BECAUSE YOU'RE *BIGGEST* DOESN'T MEAN YOU HAVE TO GO IT ALONE!
YOU SHOULD LISTEN TO YOUR SIBLING! THE BIGGER THEY ARE, THE HARDER THEY FALL!
MAYBE, BUT THEY *HIT* HARDER, TOO!
NOW WE GO...
...MAN-O-*MANOSAUR!*

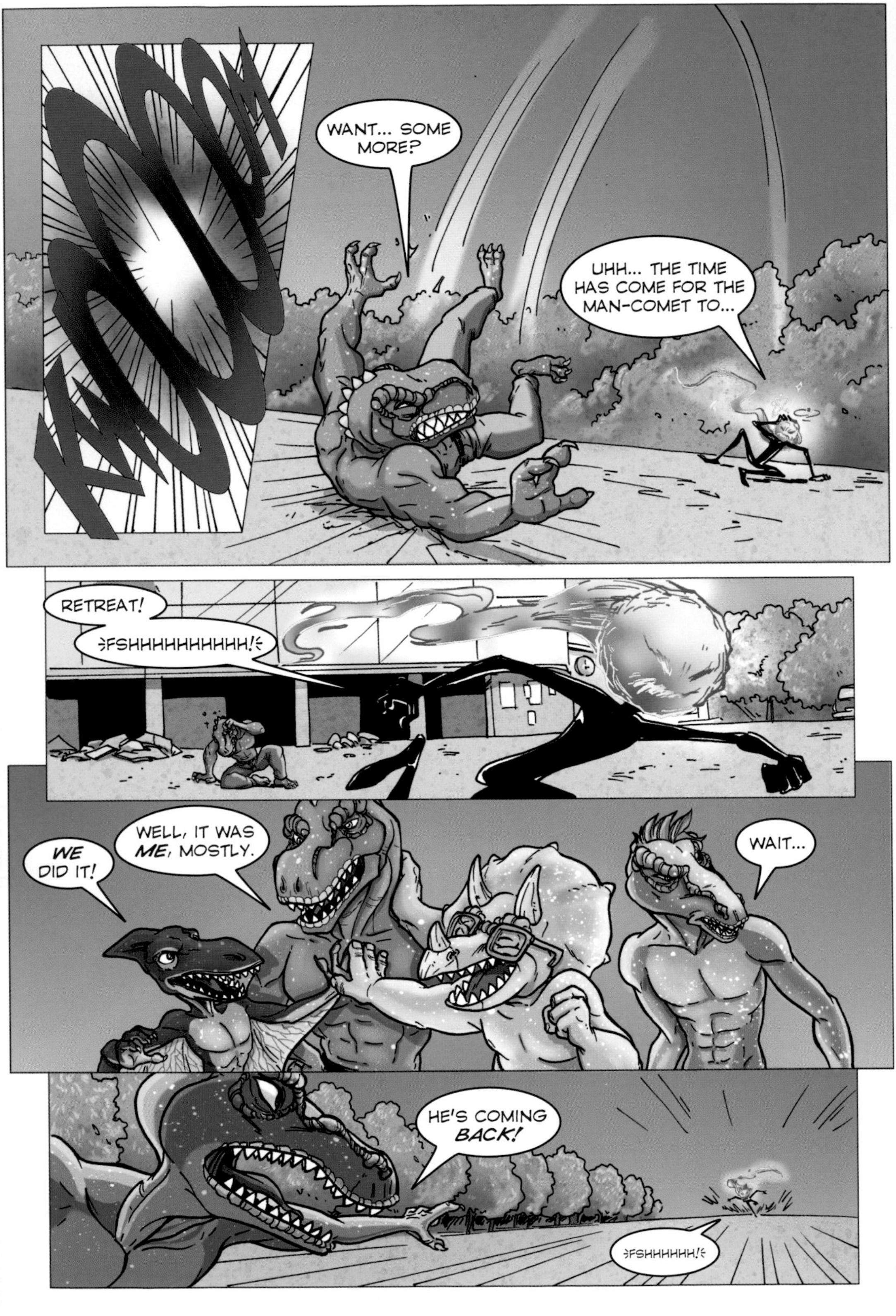
KA-BOOM
WANT... SOME MORE?
UHH... THE TIME HAS COME FOR THE MAN-COMET TO...
RETREAT!
FSHHHHHHHHHH!
WE DID IT!
WELL, IT WAS ME, MOSTLY.
WAIT...
HE'S COMING BACK!
FSHHHHHH!

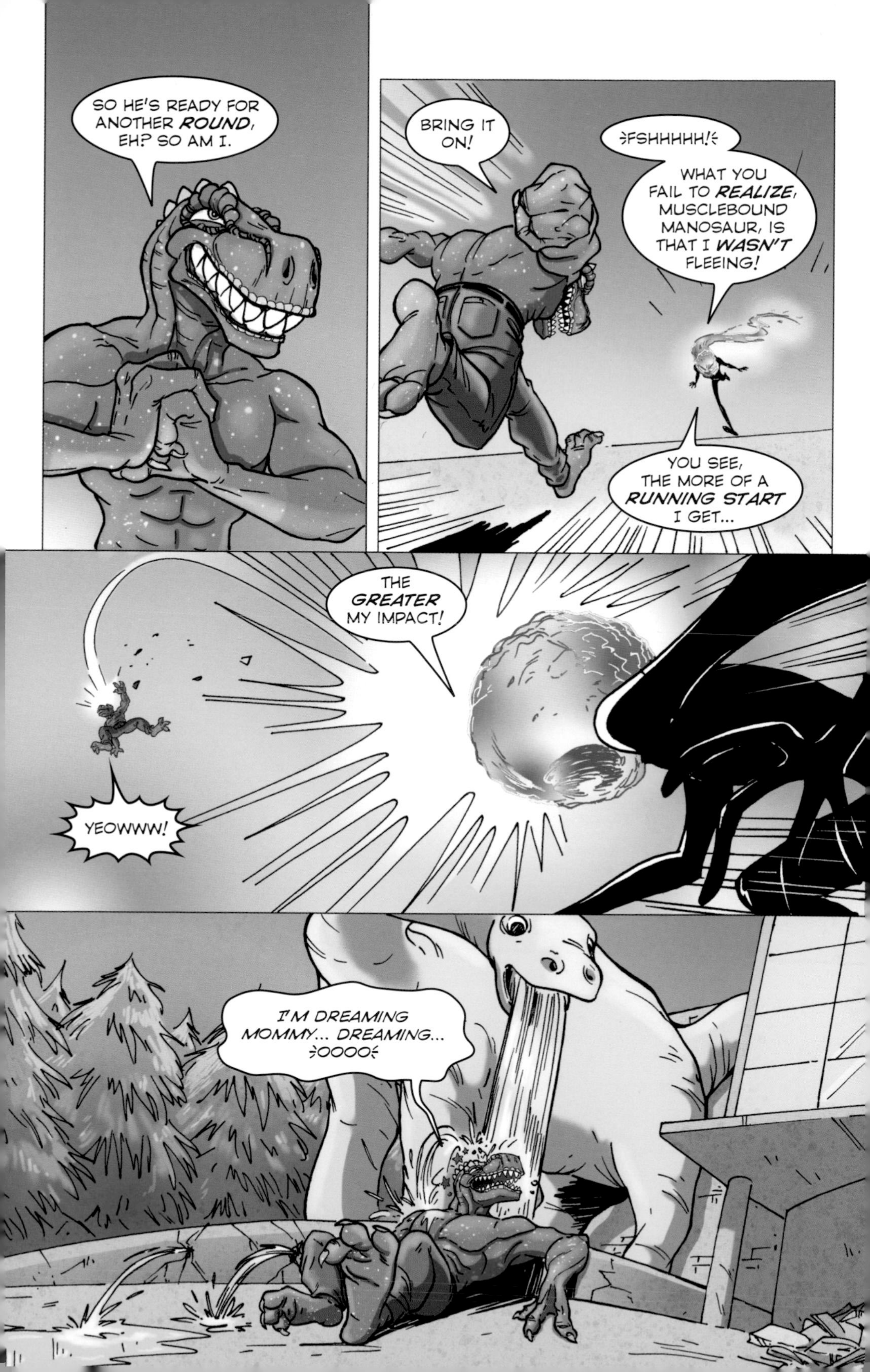
SO HE'S READY FOR ANOTHER ROUND, EH? SO AM I.
BRING IT ON!
FSHHHHH!
WHAT YOU FAIL TO REALIZE, MUSCLEBOUND MANOSAUR, IS THAT I WASN'T FLEEING!
YOU SEE, THE MORE OF A RUNNING START I GET...
THE GREATER MY IMPACT!
YEOWWW!
I'M DREAMING MOMMY... DREAMING...
OOOO

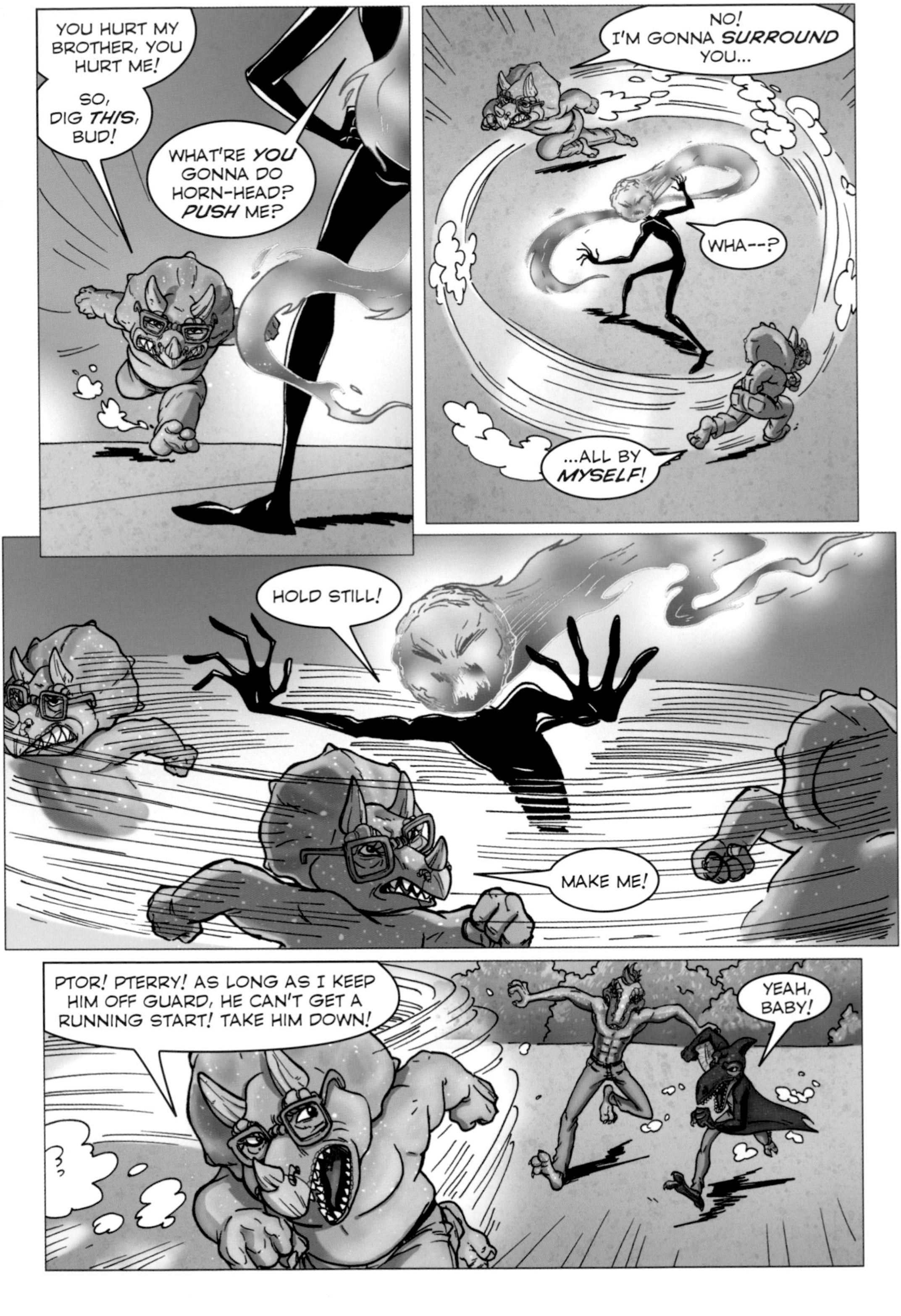
YOU HURT MY BROTHER, YOU HURT ME!
SO, DIG THIS, BUD!
WHAT'RE YOU GONNA DO HORN-HEAD? PUSH ME?
NO! I'M GONNA SURROUND YOU...
WHA--?
...ALL BY MYSELF!
HOLD STILL!
MAKE ME!
PTOR! PTERRY! AS LONG AS I KEEP HIM OFF GUARD, HE CAN'T GET A RUNNING START! TAKE HIM DOWN!
YEAH, BABY!

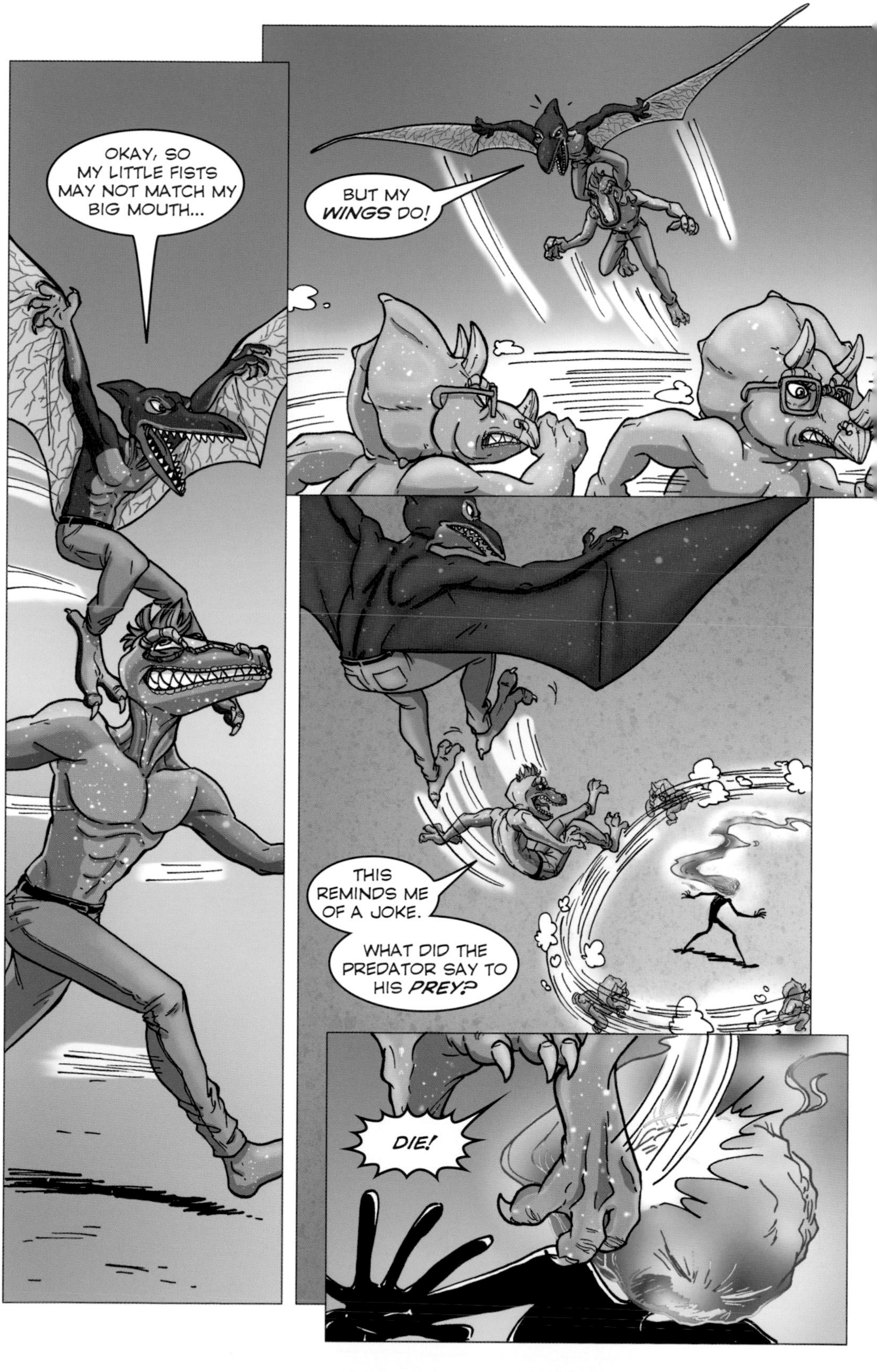
OKAY, SO MY LITTLE FISTS MAY NOT MATCH MY BIG MOUTH...
BUT MY *WINGS* DO!
THIS REMINDS ME OF A JOKE.
WHAT DID THE PREDATOR SAY TO HIS *PREY?*
DIE!

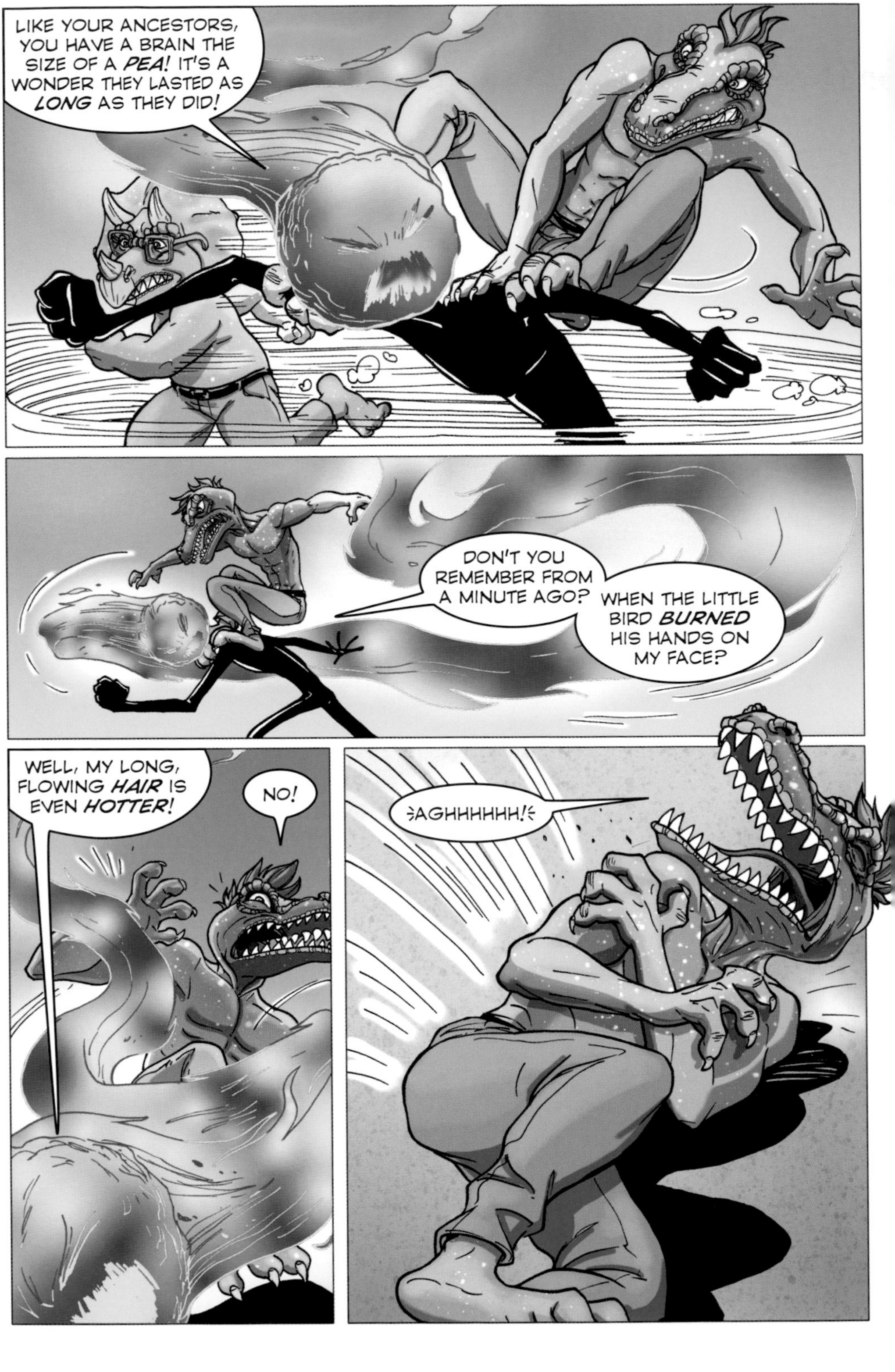
LIKE YOUR ANCESTORS, YOU HAVE A BRAIN THE SIZE OF A *PEA!* IT'S A WONDER THEY LASTED AS *LONG* AS THEY DID!
DON'T YOU REMEMBER FROM A MINUTE AGO?
WHEN THE LITTLE BIRD *BURNED* HIS HANDS ON MY FACE?
WELL, MY LONG, FLOWING *HAIR* IS EVEN *HOTTER!*
NO!
AGHHHHHH!

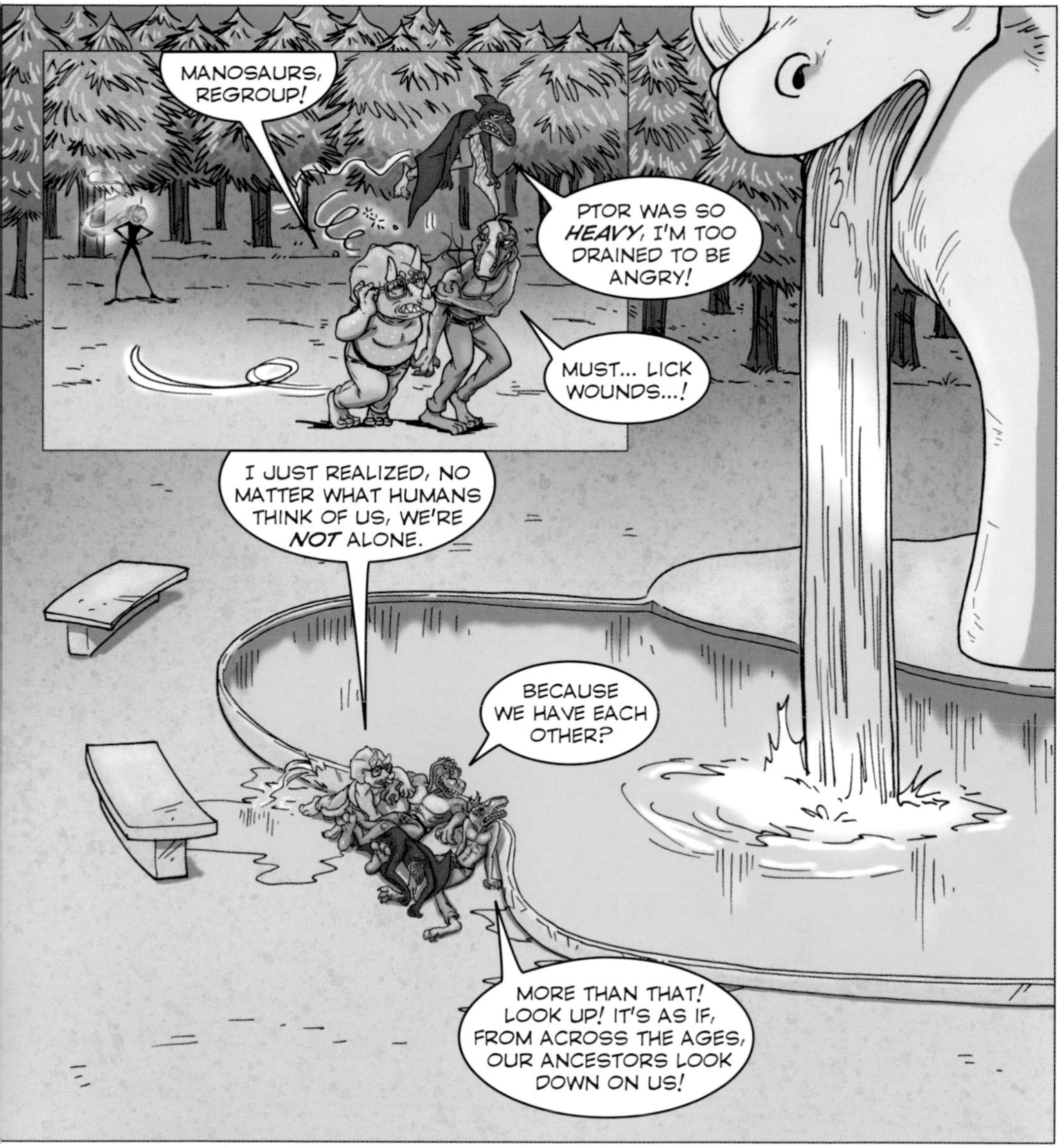
MANOSAURS, REGROUP!
PTOR WAS SO HEAVY, I'M TOO DRAINED TO BE ANGRY!
MUST... LICK WOUNDS...!
I JUST REALIZED, NO MATTER WHAT HUMANS THINK OF US, WE'RE NOT ALONE.
BECAUSE WE HAVE EACH OTHER?
MORE THAN THAT! LOOK UP! IT'S AS IF, FROM ACROSS THE AGES, OUR ANCESTORS LOOK DOWN ON US!

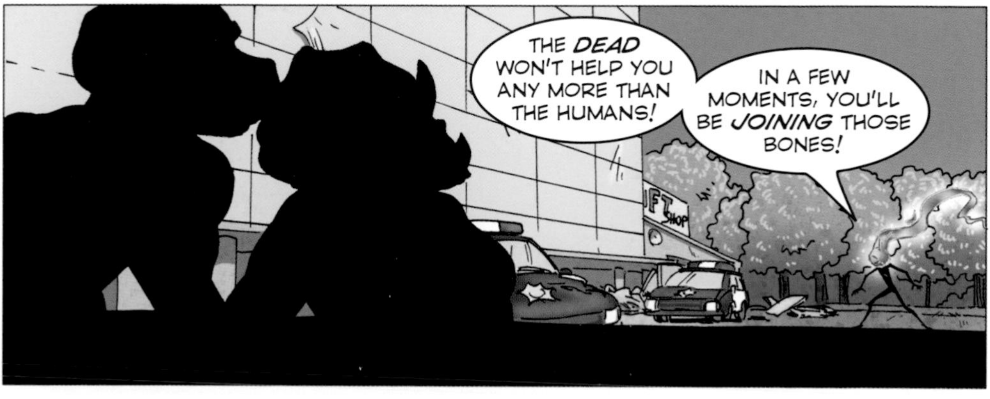
THE DEAD WON'T HELP YOU ANY MORE THAN THE HUMANS!
IN A FEW MOMENTS, YOU'LL BE JOINING THOSE BONES!

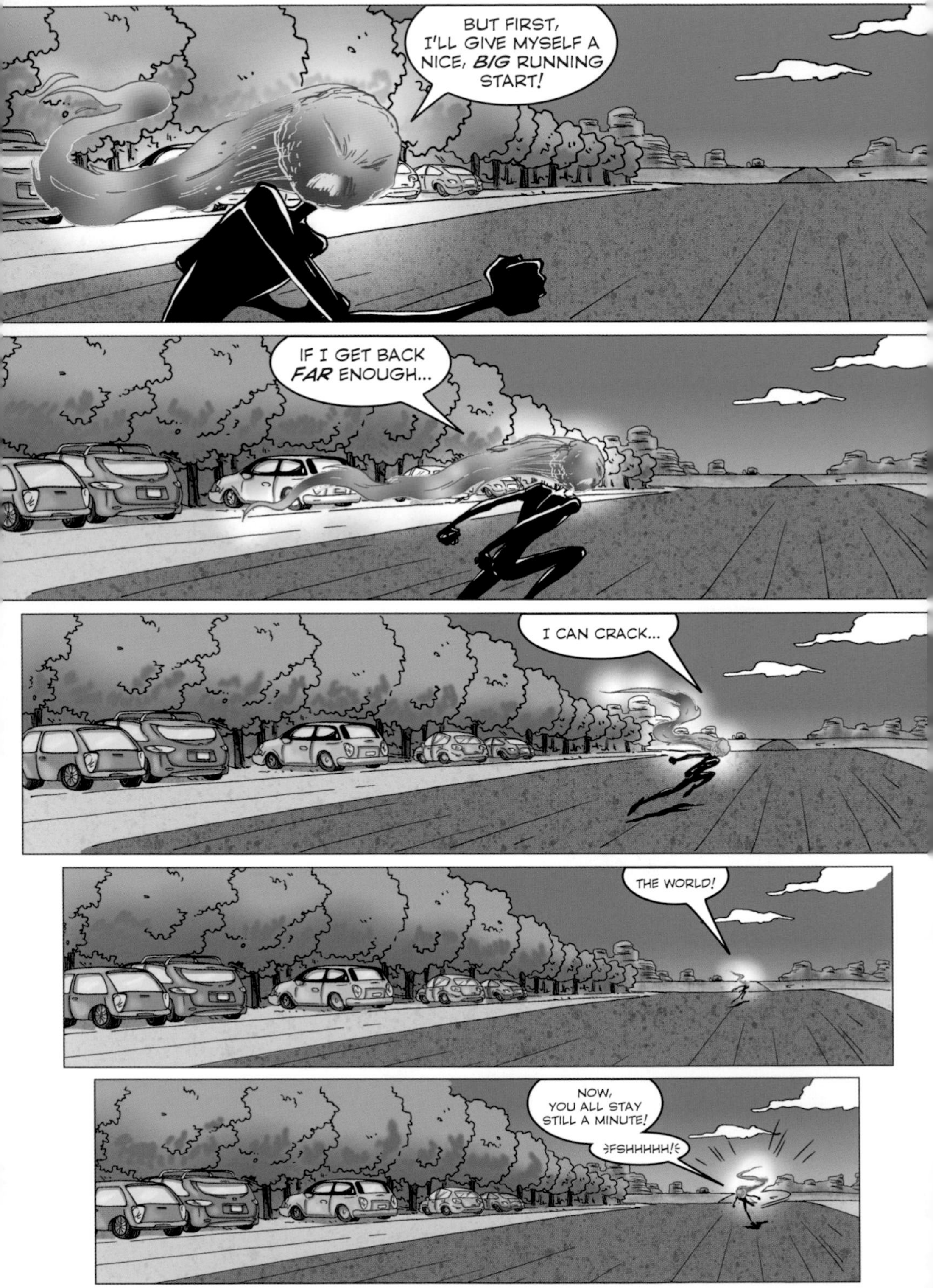
BUT FIRST, I'LL GIVE MYSELF A NICE, BIG RUNNING START!
IF I GET BACK FAR ENOUGH...
I CAN CRACK...
THE WORLD!
NOW, YOU ALL STAY STILL A MINUTE!
FSHHHHH!

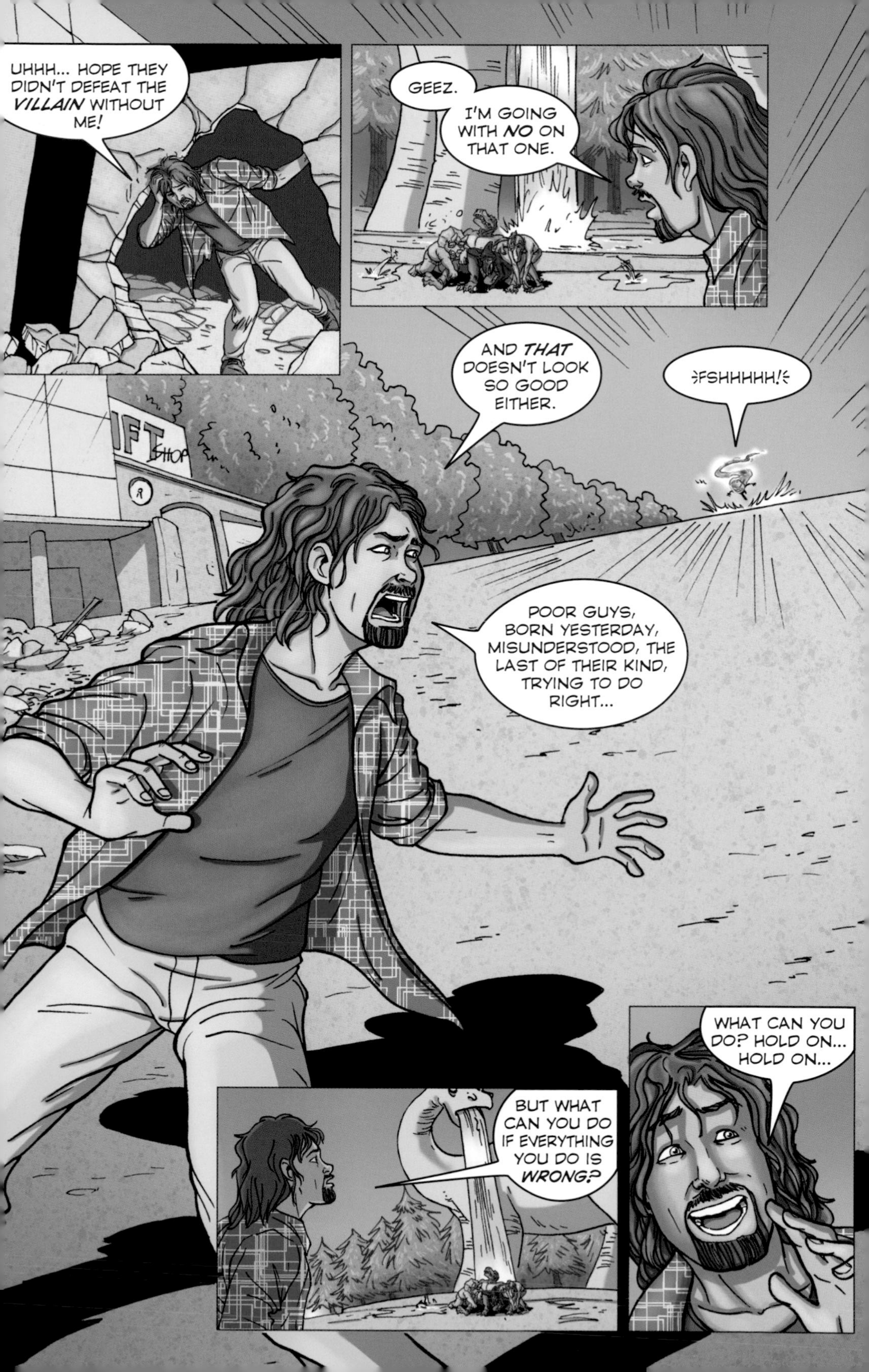
UHHH... HOPE THEY DIDN'T DEFEAT THE *VILLAIN* WITHOUT ME!
GEEZ.
I'M GOING WITH *NO* ON THAT ONE.
AND *THAT* DOESN'T LOOK SO GOOD EITHER.
FSHHHHH!
IFT SHOP
POOR GUYS, BORN YESTERDAY, MISUNDERSTOOD, THE LAST OF THEIR KIND, TRYING TO DO RIGHT...
BUT WHAT CAN YOU DO IF EVERYTHING YOU DO IS *WRONG?*
WHAT CAN YOU DO? HOLD ON... HOLD ON...

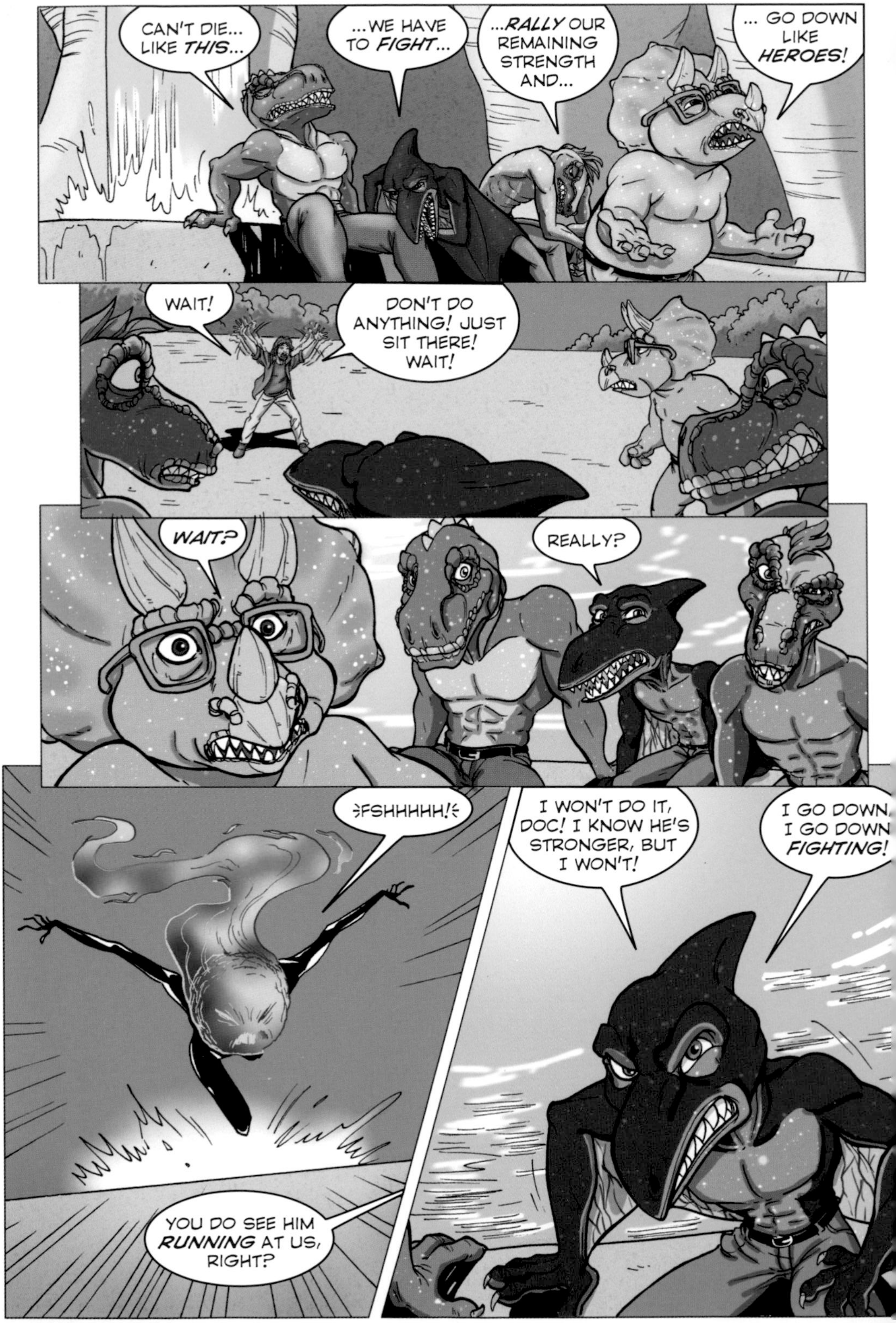
CAN'T DIE... LIKE THIS...
...WE HAVE TO FIGHT...
...RALLY OUR REMAINING STRENGTH AND...
... GO DOWN LIKE HEROES!
WAIT!
DON'T DO ANYTHING! JUST SIT THERE! WAIT!
WAIT?
REALLY?
FSHHHHH!
YOU DO SEE HIM RUNNING AT US, RIGHT?
I WON'T DO IT, DOC! I KNOW HE'S STRONGER, BUT I WON'T!
I GO DOWN, I GO DOWN FIGHTING!

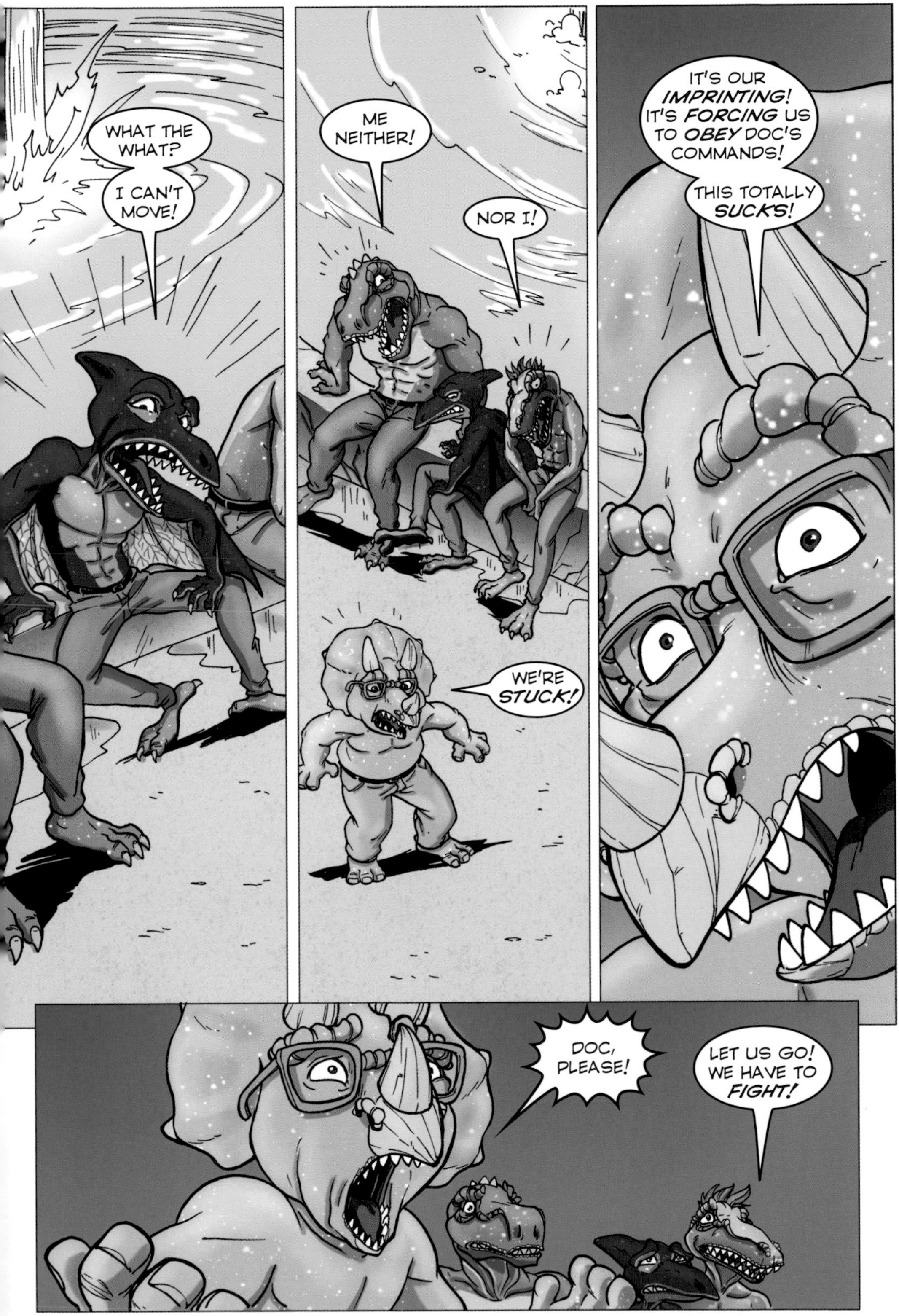
WHAT THE WHAT?
I CAN'T MOVE!
ME NEITHER!
NOR I!
WE'RE STUCK!
IT'S OUR IMPRINTING! IT'S FORCING US TO OBEY DOC'S COMMANDS!
THIS TOTALLY SUCKS!
DOC, PLEASE!
LET US GO! WE HAVE TO FIGHT!

BET EVERY PARENT WISHES THAT'D WORK!

NO, TRI, *TRUST* ME. KEEP WAITING.

"WAIT. WAIT.

⇂FSHHHHH!⇃

"WAIIIITTTTT.

⇂FSHHHHH!⇃

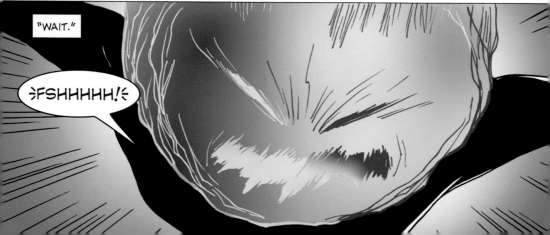

"WAIT."

⇂FSHHHHH!⇃

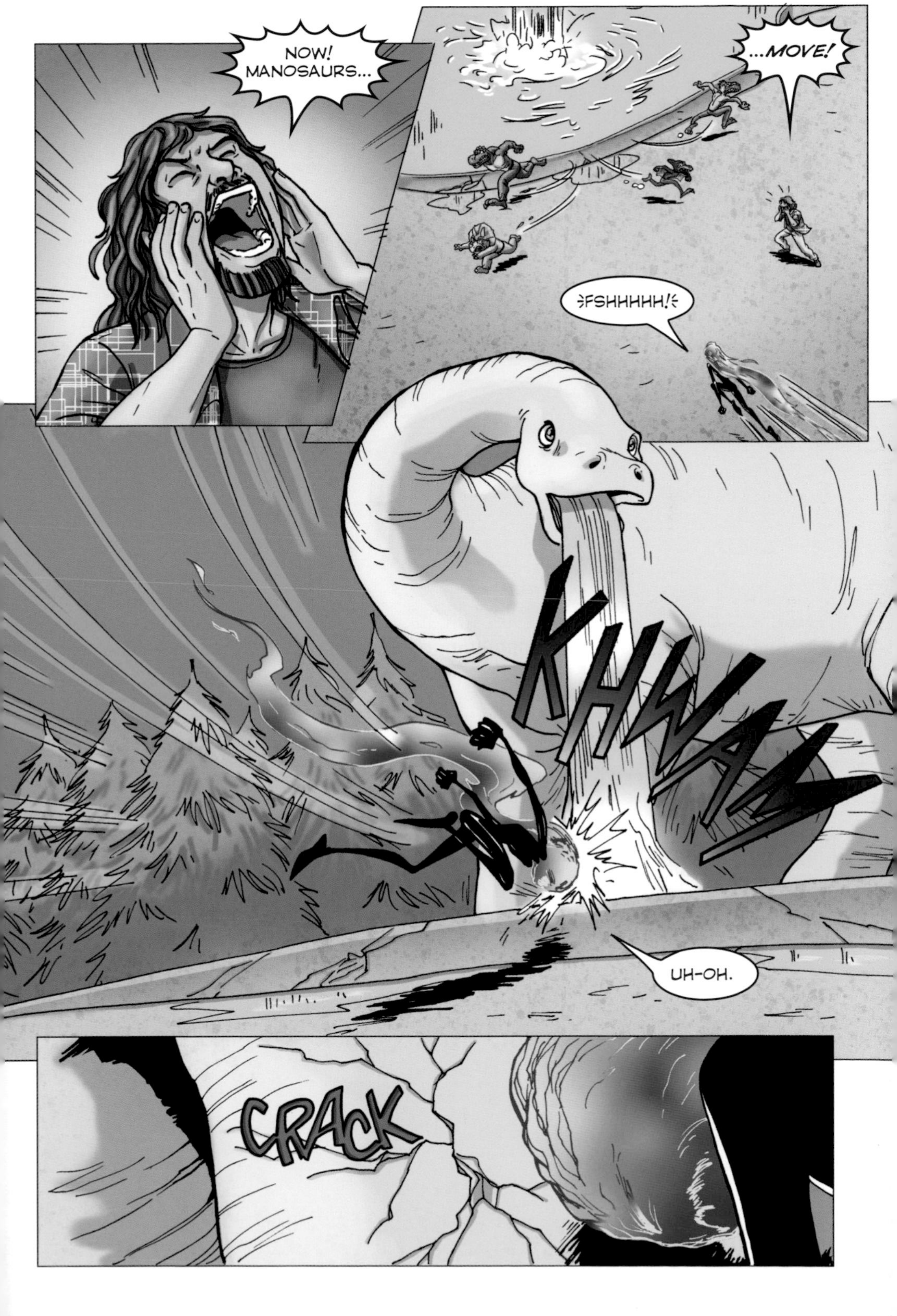
NOW! MANOSAURS...
...MOVE!
FSHHHHH!
KHWAM
UH-OH.
CRACK

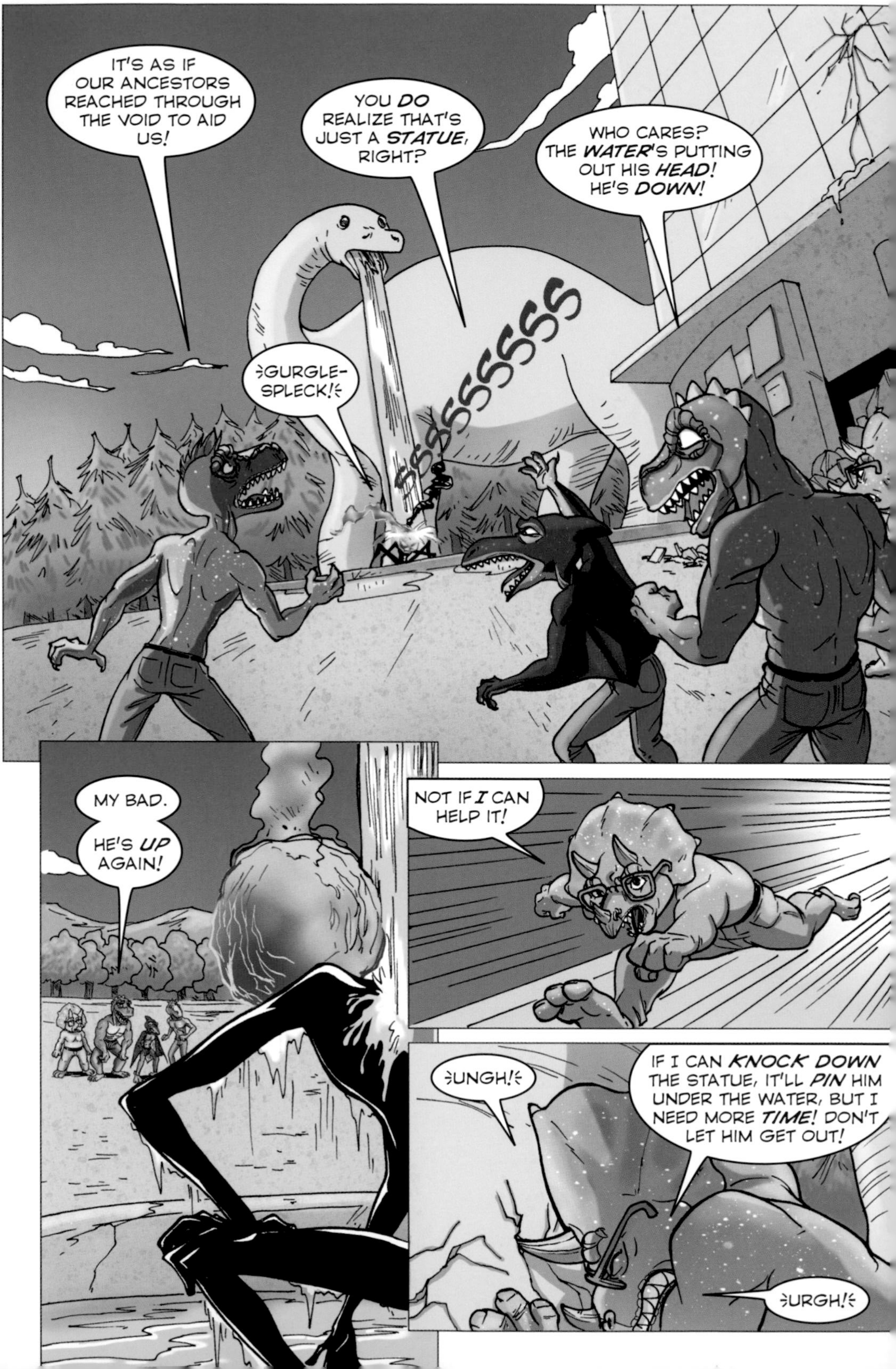
IT'S AS IF OUR ANCESTORS REACHED THROUGH THE VOID TO AID US!
YOU DO REALIZE THAT'S JUST A STATUE, RIGHT?
WHO CARES? THE WATER'S PUTTING OUT HIS HEAD! HE'S DOWN!
SSSSSSSSSSS
GURGLE-SPLECK!
MY BAD.
HE'S UP AGAIN!
NOT IF I CAN HELP IT!
UNGH!
IF I CAN KNOCK DOWN THE STATUE, IT'LL PIN HIM UNDER THE WATER, BUT I NEED MORE TIME! DON'T LET HIM GET OUT!
URGH!

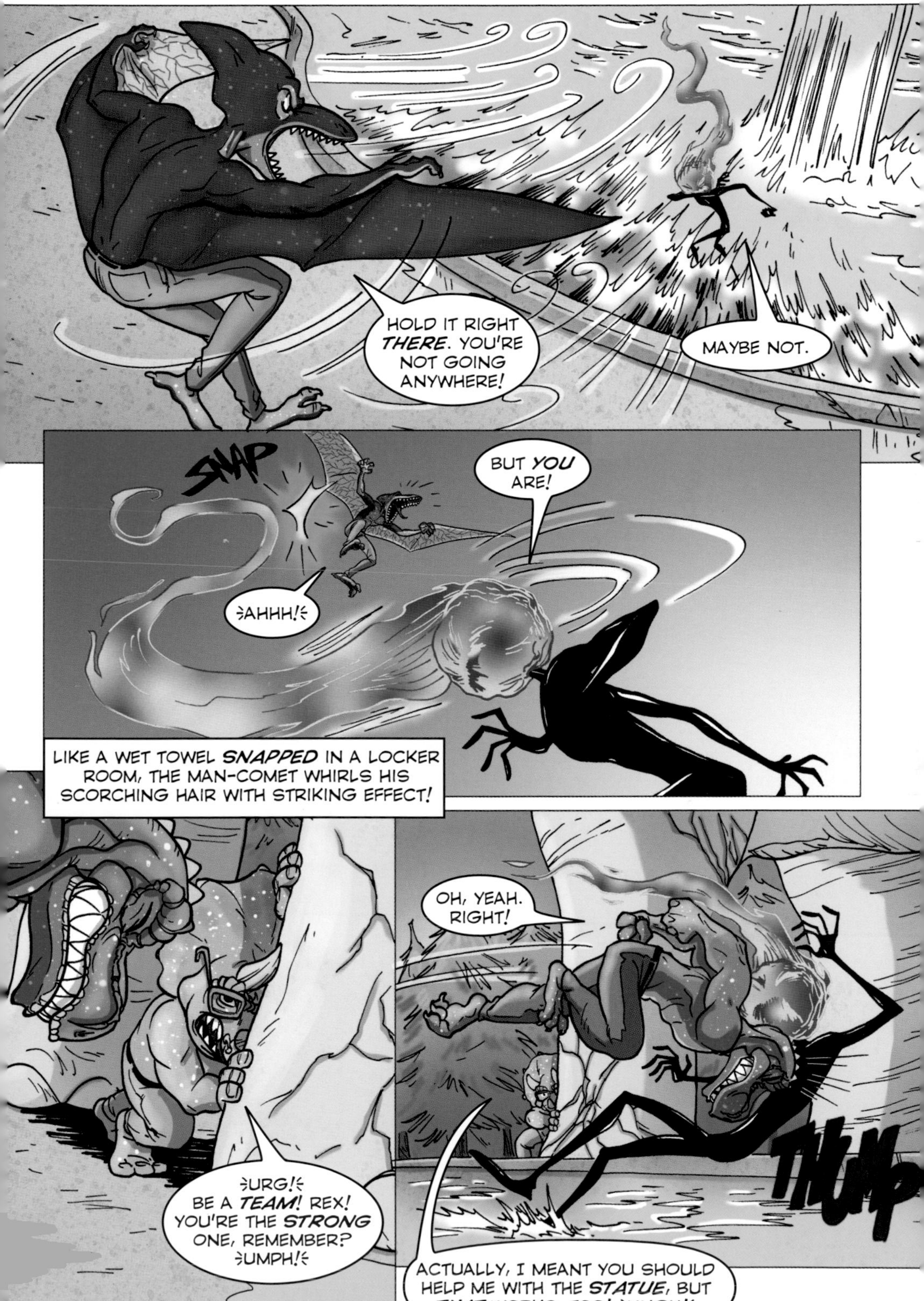
HOLD IT RIGHT THERE. YOU'RE NOT GOING ANYWHERE!
MAYBE NOT.
SNAP
BUT YOU ARE!
AHHH!
LIKE A WET TOWEL SNAPPED IN A LOCKER ROOM, THE MAN-COMET WHIRLS HIS SCORCHING HAIR WITH STRIKING EFFECT!
URG! BE A TEAM! REX! YOU'RE THE STRONG ONE, REMEMBER? UMPH!
OH, YEAH. RIGHT!
THUMP
ACTUALLY, I MEANT YOU SHOULD HELP ME WITH THE STATUE, BUT THAT WORKS, TOO! UNGH!

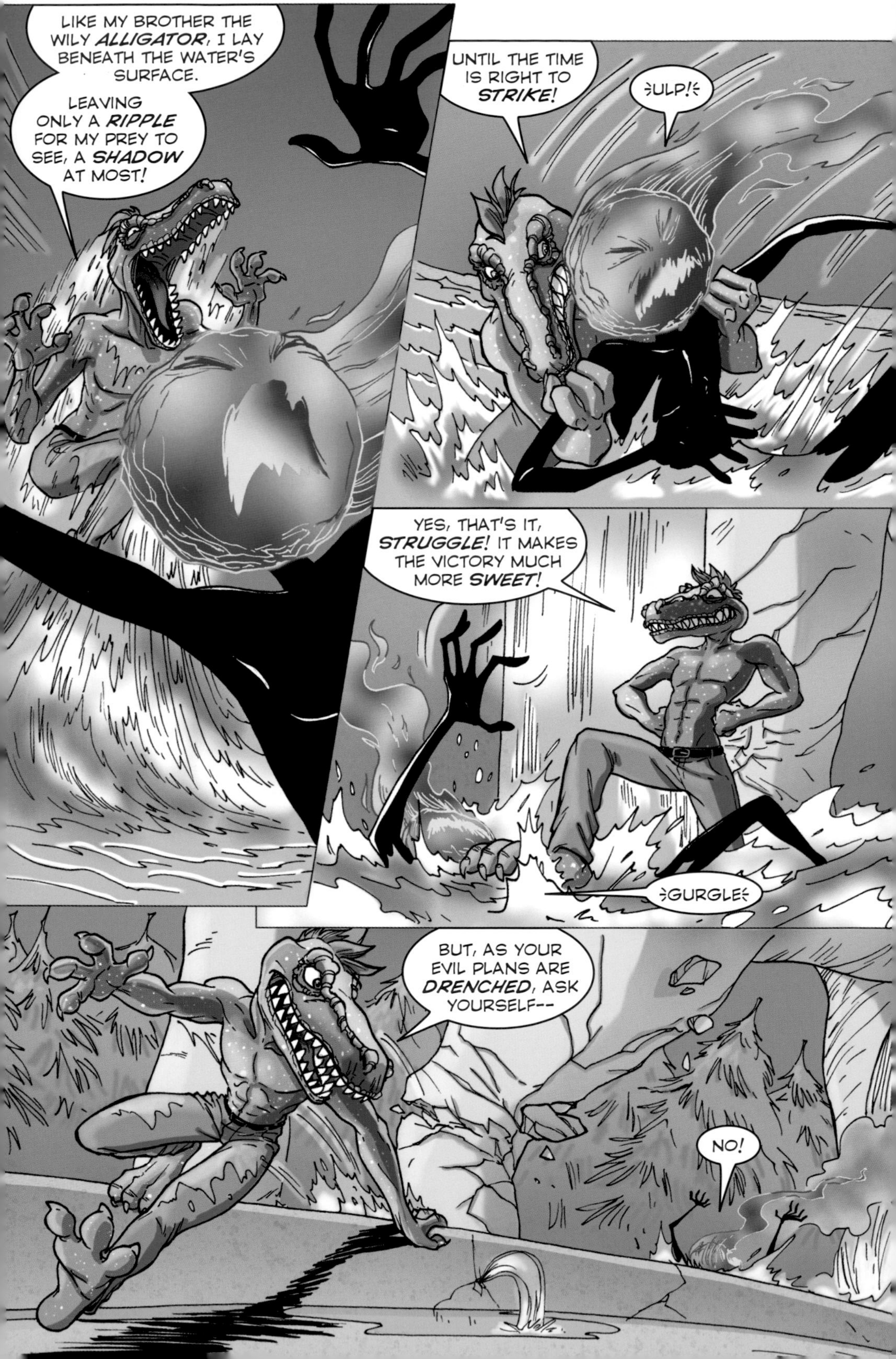
LIKE MY BROTHER THE WILY ALLIGATOR, I LAY BENEATH THE WATER'S SURFACE.
LEAVING ONLY A RIPPLE FOR MY PREY TO SEE, A SHADOW AT MOST!
UNTIL THE TIME IS RIGHT TO STRIKE!
ULP!
YES, THAT'S IT, STRUGGLE! IT MAKES THE VICTORY MUCH MORE SWEET!
GURGLE
BUT, AS YOUR EVIL PLANS ARE DRENCHED, ASK YOURSELF--
NO!

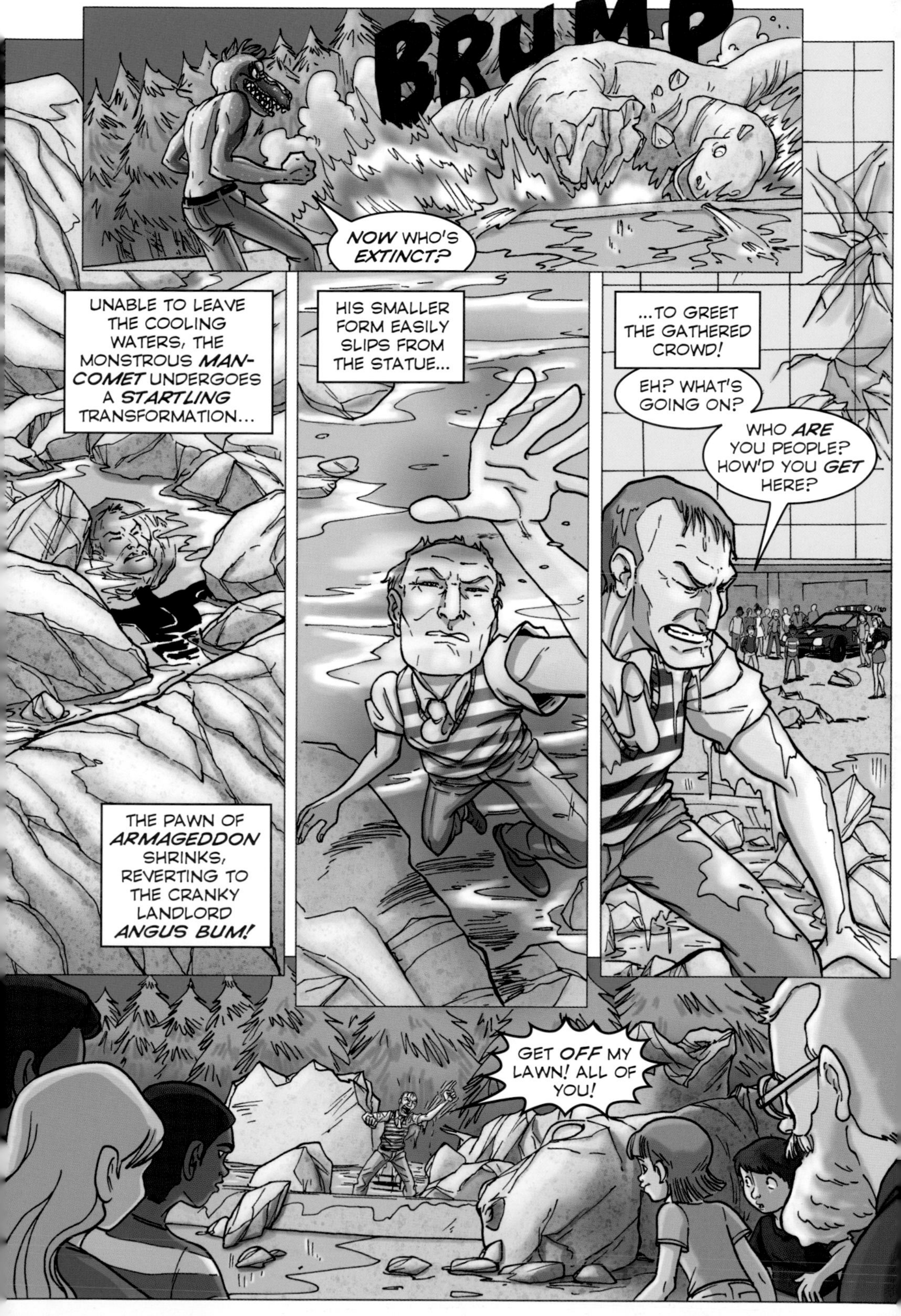
BRUMP
NOW WHO'S EXTINCT?
UNABLE TO LEAVE THE COOLING WATERS, THE MONSTROUS MAN-COMET UNDERGOES A STARTLING TRANSFORMATION...
THE PAWN OF ARMAGEDDON SHRINKS, REVERTING TO THE CRANKY LANDLORD ANGUS BUM!
HIS SMALLER FORM EASILY SLIPS FROM THE STATUE...
...TO GREET THE GATHERED CROWD!
EH? WHAT'S GOING ON?
WHO ARE YOU PEOPLE? HOW'D YOU GET HERE?
GET OFF MY LAWN! ALL OF YOU!

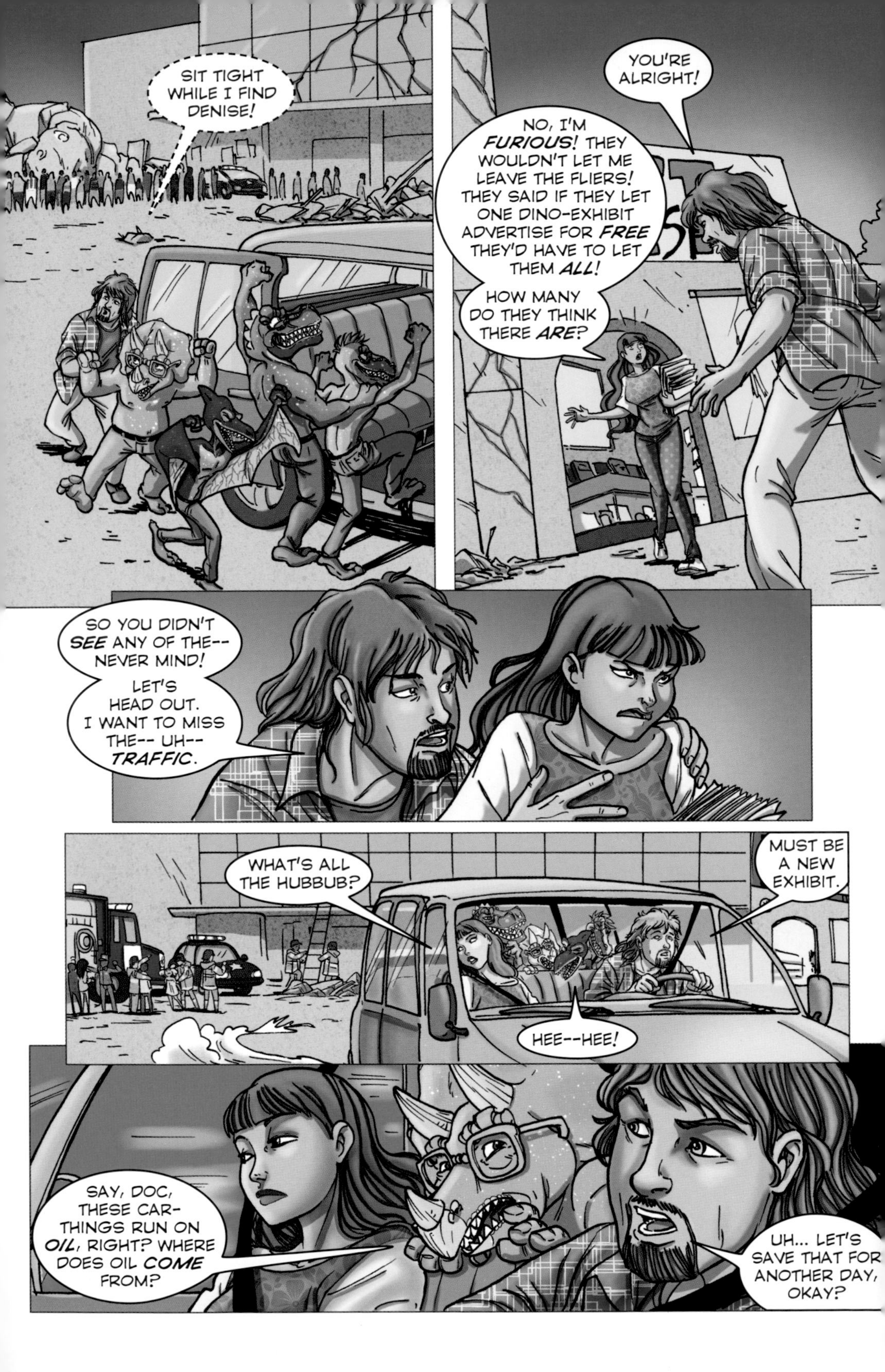
SIT TIGHT WHILE I FIND DENISE!
YOU'RE ALRIGHT!
NO, I'M FURIOUS! THEY WOULDN'T LET ME LEAVE THE FLIERS! THEY SAID IF THEY LET ONE DINO-EXHIBIT ADVERTISE FOR FREE THEY'D HAVE TO LET THEM ALL!
HOW MANY DO THEY THINK THERE ARE?
SO YOU DIDN'T SEE ANY OF THE-- NEVER MIND!
LET'S HEAD OUT. I WANT TO MISS THE-- UH-- TRAFFIC.
WHAT'S ALL THE HUBBUB?
MUST BE A NEW EXHIBIT.
HEE--HEE!
SAY, DOC, THESE CAR-THINGS RUN ON OIL, RIGHT? WHERE DOES OIL COME FROM?
UH... LET'S SAVE THAT FOR ANOTHER DAY, OKAY?

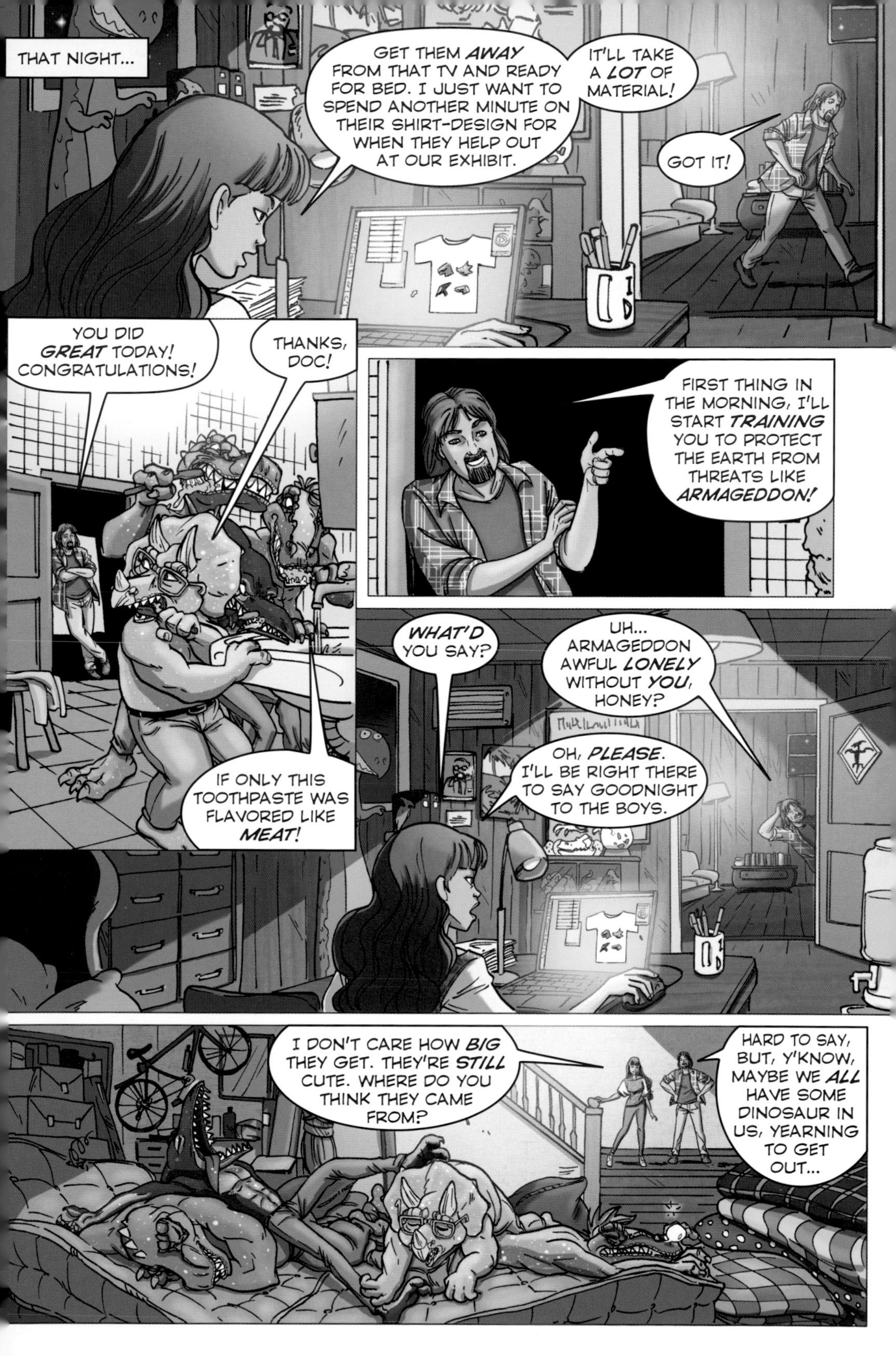
THAT NIGHT...
GET THEM *AWAY* FROM THAT TV AND READY FOR BED. I JUST WANT TO SPEND ANOTHER MINUTE ON THEIR SHIRT-DESIGN FOR WHEN THEY HELP OUT AT OUR EXHIBIT.
IT'LL TAKE A *LOT* OF MATERIAL!
GOT IT!
YOU DID *GREAT* TODAY! CONGRATULATIONS!
THANKS, DOC!
IF ONLY THIS TOOTHPASTE WAS FLAVORED LIKE *MEAT*!
FIRST THING IN THE MORNING, I'LL START *TRAINING* YOU TO PROTECT THE EARTH FROM THREATS LIKE *ARMAGEDDON!*
WHAT'D YOU SAY?
UH... ARMAGEDDON AWFUL *LONELY* WITHOUT *YOU*, HONEY?
OH, *PLEASE*. I'LL BE RIGHT THERE TO SAY GOODNIGHT TO THE BOYS.
I DON'T CARE HOW *BIG* THEY GET. THEY'RE *STILL* CUTE. WHERE DO YOU THINK THEY CAME FROM?
HARD TO SAY, BUT, Y'KNOW, MAYBE WE *ALL* HAVE SOME DINOSAUR IN US, YEARNING TO GET OUT...

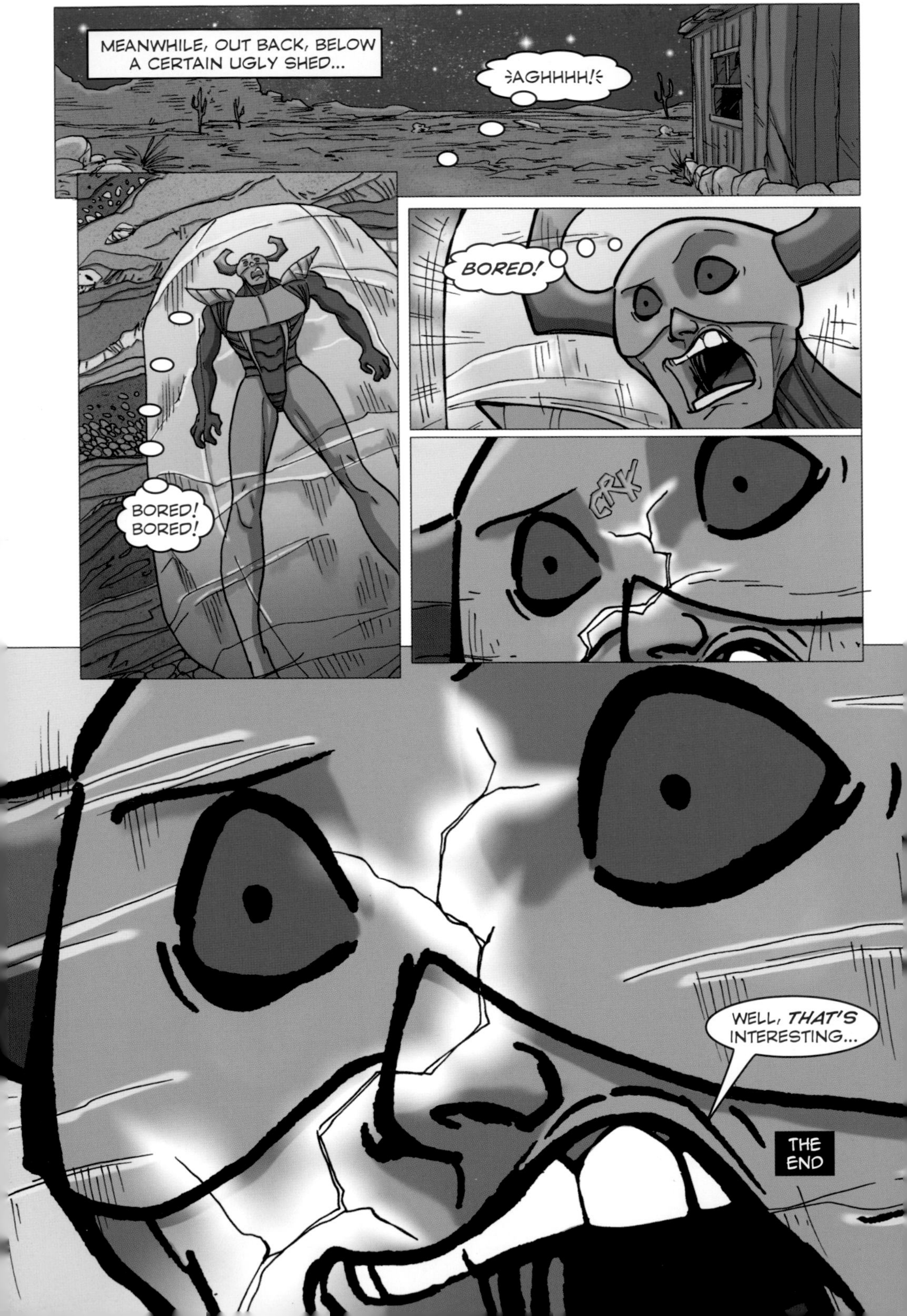
MEANWHILE, OUT BACK, BELOW A CERTAIN UGLY SHED...
AGHHHH!
BORED! BORED!
BORED!
CRK
WELL, *THAT'S* INTERESTING...
THE END

WATCH OUT FOR PAPERCUTZ

Welcome to the post-historic, premiere MANOSAURS graphic novel, based on the comicbook series created by Stuart Fischer, written by Stefan Petrucha, and illustrated by Yellowhale Studios, from Papercutz—those amateur paleontologists dedicated to publishing great graphic novels for all ages (not just the Jurassic!). I'm Jim Salicrup, Editor-in-Chief and Fossil Fool, here to ramble about MANOSAURS and Papercutz…

While dinosaurs existed between from about 230 million years ago up until about 65 million years ago, MANOSAURS are a relatively new thing. They were first discovered in 1993 in two MANOSAURS comicbooks, #0 and #1. The MANOSAURS are created by Stuart Fischer, a man I've met just a few times, and who I mostly remember for his connection to *Mutt and Jeff* and his *Green Lantern* ring. Stuart's a clever guy, and the idea of creatures that combine the relative strengths of humans (intelligence) and dinosaurs (strength) is so good, you have to wonder why no one else ever thought of it. I'm hoping this new incarnation of MANOSAURS becomes a huge hit, not only because I want Papercutz to publish as many super-successful graphic novels as possible, but I secretly want my original MANOSAURS comicbooks to become valuable ($$) collector's items.

STEFAN PETRUCHA
ALLEN GLADFELTER
HOTEL TRANSYLVANIA
ALL-NEW GRAPHIC NOVEL BASED ON THE HIT MOVIES!
KAKIELAND KATASTROPHE
PAPERCUTZ

Plumeri & Bloz
Dinosaurs
IN THE BEGINNING...
PAPERCUTZ

Dinosaures [DINOSAURS] by Arnaud Plumeri & Bloz

Guiding the MANOSAURS back to comicbook life is none other Stefan Petrucha, a writer who has been with Papercutz since the beginning, writing such titles for us as NANCY DREW DIARIES, POWER RANGERS, RIO, MICKEY'S INFERNO, and HOTEL TRANSYLVANIA. Stefan has written all sorts of comics over the years, such as *The X-Files*, *Donald Duck*, *Meta-4*, *Lance Barnes*, *Post Nuke Dick*, *Squalor*, and was even nominated for a Bram Stoker Award for the graphic novel, *Kolchak Night Stalker: Devil in the Details*. Stefan's also written tons of books, including such YA series as *Timetripper*, *Rule of Won*, *Split*, plus *Dead Mann Walking*, *Ripper*, *The Shadow of Frankenstein*, as well as novels starring *Captain America*, *Deadpool*, and *Spider-Man*. For a peek at his latest Papercutz project, check out the preview of HOTEL TRANSYLVANIA on the following pages.

Believe it or not, this isn't the first time Papercutz has published a graphic novel series with talking dinosaurs. Take a look at the preview pages from DINOSAURS, by Arnaud Plumeri and Bloz, to get a taste of what that fact-filled series is like. Before I get too carried away, let me remind you that you can find out about all the available graphic novels we publish at papercutz.com. There may even be a peek at MANOSAURS #2 "The Horrific, Dreadful, Awful, Terror of Thesaurus—The Thing with Many Names!" So on that note, allow me to say good-bye, farewell, so long, adieu, aloha, adios, ta-ta!

Thanks, Jim

STAY IN TOUCH!

EMAIL:	salicrup@papercutz.com
WEB:	www.papercutz.com
TWITTER:	@papercutzgn
INSTAGRAM:	@papercutzgn
FACEBOOK:	PAPERCUTZGRAPHICNOVELS
REGULAR MAIL:	Papercutz, 160 Broadway, Suite 700, East Wing, New York, NY 10038

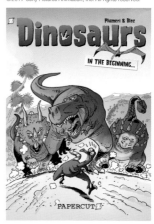

Special Preview of HOTEL TRANSYLVANIA #1 "Kakieland Katastrophe"...

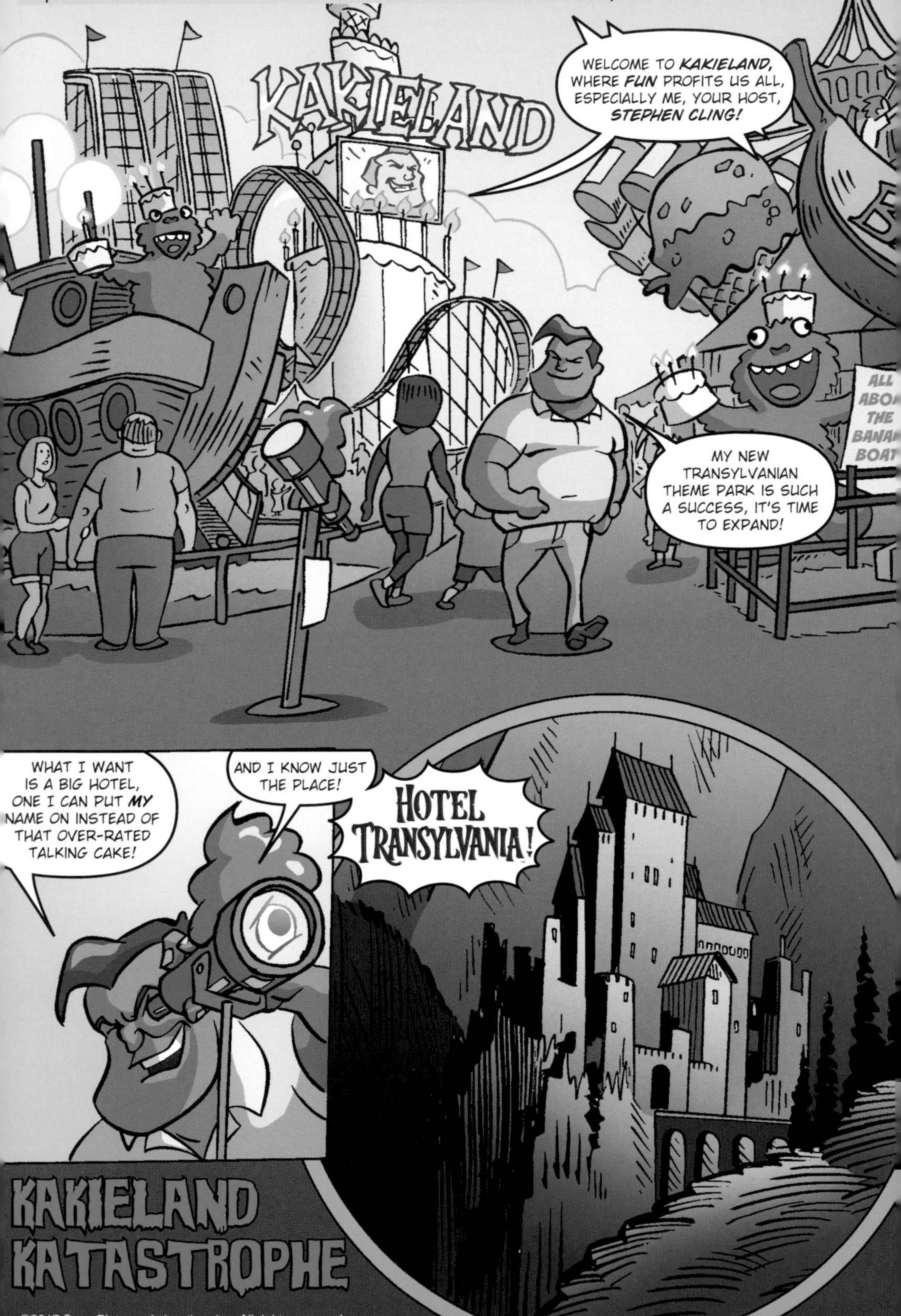

KAKIELAND
WELCOME TO KAKIELAND, WHERE FUN PROFITS US ALL, ESPECIALLY ME, YOUR HOST, STEPHEN CLING!
MY NEW TRANSYLVANIAN THEME PARK IS SUCH A SUCCESS, IT'S TIME TO EXPAND!
WHAT I WANT IS A BIG HOTEL, ONE I CAN PUT MY NAME ON INSTEAD OF THAT OVER-RATED TALKING CAKE!
AND I KNOW JUST THE PLACE!
HOTEL TRANSYLVANIA!
KAKIELAND KATASTROPHE

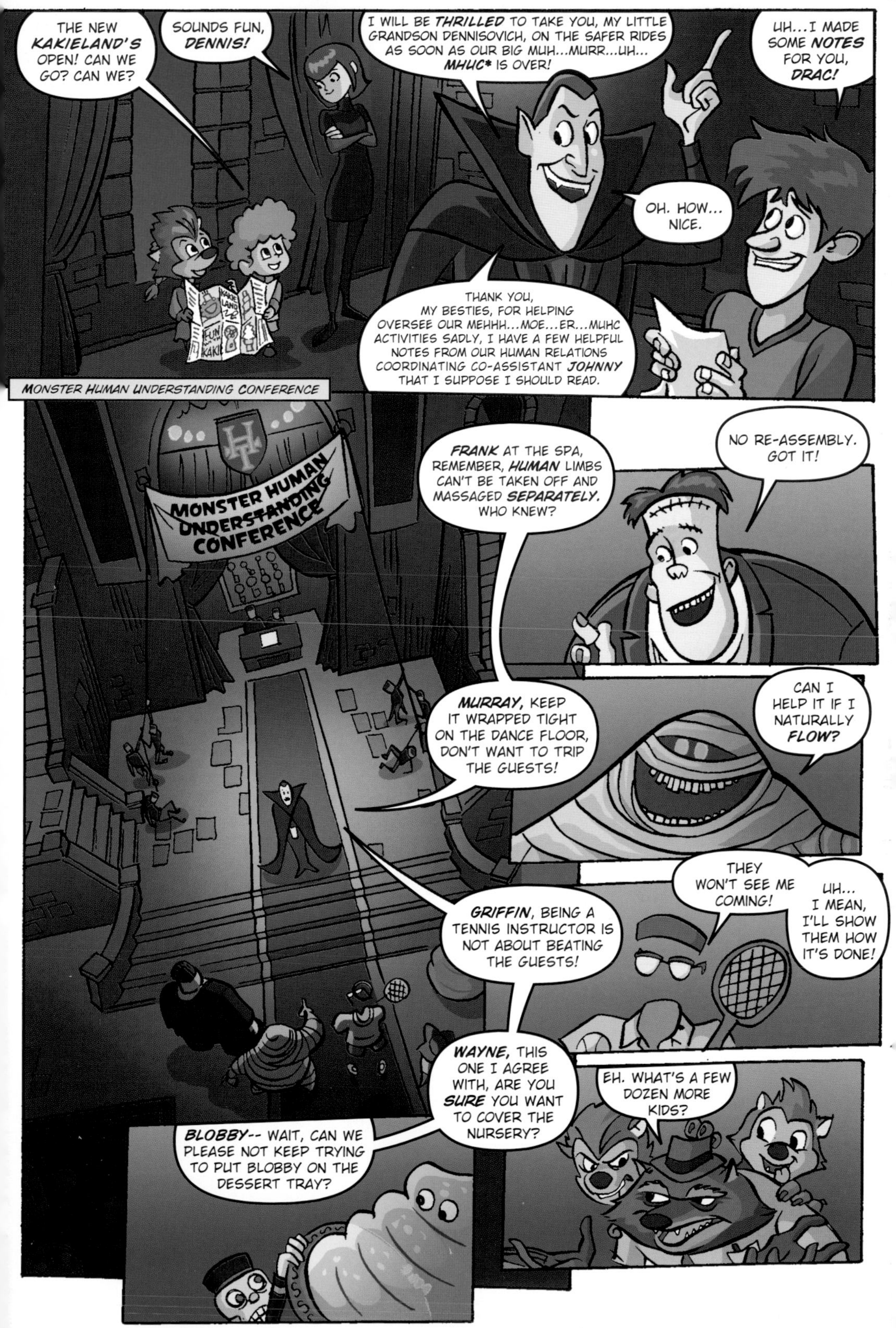
THE NEW KAKIELAND'S OPEN! CAN WE GO? CAN WE?
SOUNDS FUN, DENNIS!
I WILL BE THRILLED TO TAKE YOU, MY LITTLE GRANDSON DENNISOVICH, ON THE SAFER RIDES AS SOON AS OUR BIG MUH...MURR...UH... MHUC* IS OVER!
UH...I MADE SOME NOTES FOR YOU, DRAC!
OH. HOW... NICE.
THANK YOU, MY BESTIES, FOR HELPING OVERSEE OUR MEHHH...MOE...ER...MUHC ACTIVITIES SADLY, I HAVE A FEW HELPFUL NOTES FROM OUR HUMAN RELATIONS COORDINATING CO-ASSISTANT JOHNNY THAT I SUPPOSE I SHOULD READ.
MONSTER HUMAN UNDERSTANDING CONFERENCE
MONSTER HUMAN UNDERSTANDING CONFERENCE
FRANK AT THE SPA, REMEMBER, HUMAN LIMBS CAN'T BE TAKEN OFF AND MASSAGED SEPARATELY. WHO KNEW?
NO RE-ASSEMBLY. GOT IT!
MURRAY, KEEP IT WRAPPED TIGHT ON THE DANCE FLOOR, DON'T WANT TO TRIP THE GUESTS!
CAN I HELP IT IF I NATURALLY FLOW?
GRIFFIN, BEING A TENNIS INSTRUCTOR IS NOT ABOUT BEATING THE GUESTS!
THEY WON'T SEE ME COMING!
UH... I MEAN, I'LL SHOW THEM HOW IT'S DONE!
WAYNE, THIS ONE I AGREE WITH, ARE YOU SURE YOU WANT TO COVER THE NURSERY?
EH. WHAT'S A FEW DOZEN MORE KIDS?
BLOBBY-- WAIT, CAN WE PLEASE NOT KEEP TRYING TO PUT BLOBBY ON THE DESSERT TRAY?

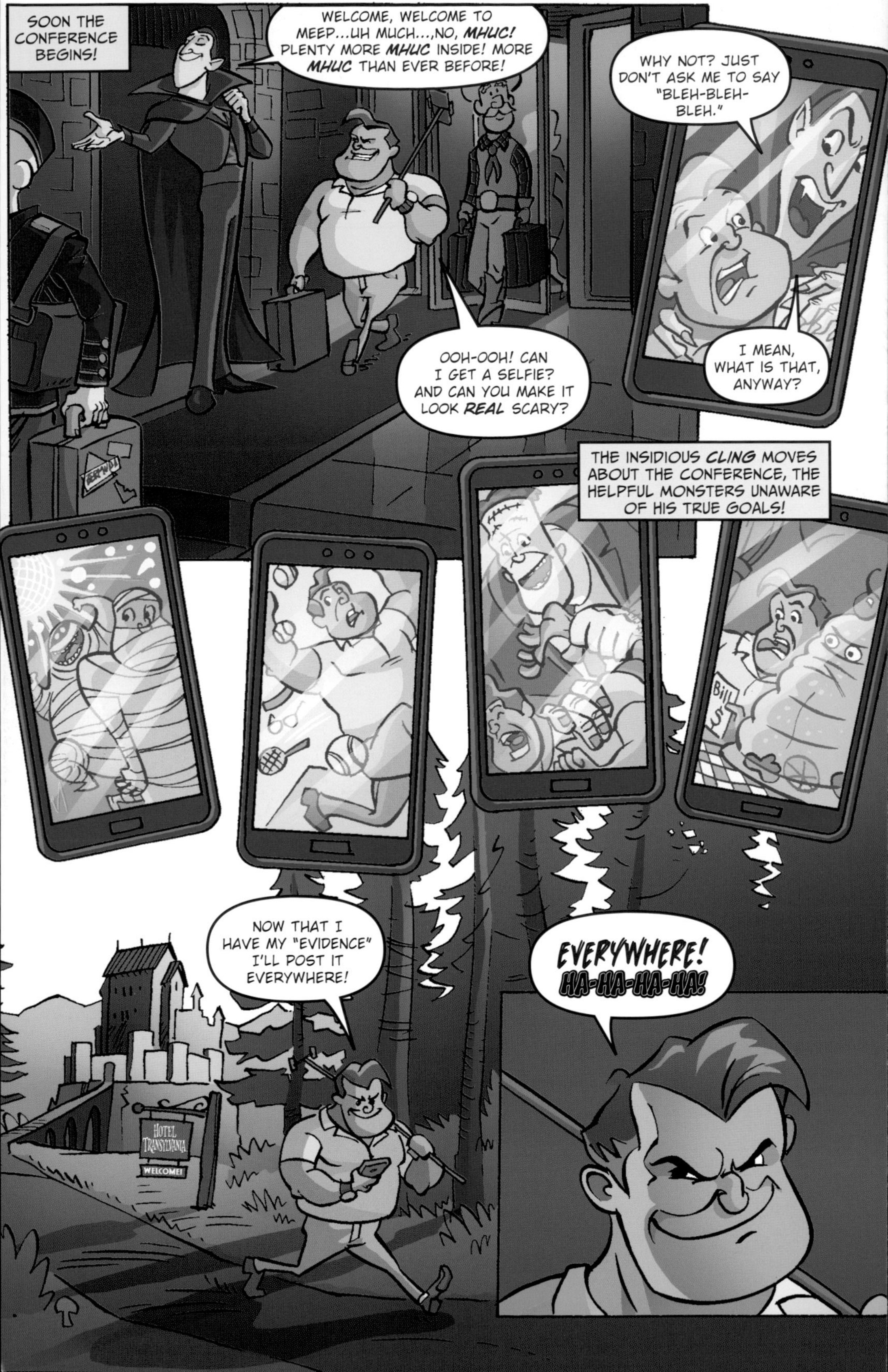
SOON THE CONFERENCE BEGINS!
WELCOME, WELCOME TO MEEP...UH MUCH...,NO, MHUC! PLENTY MORE MHUC INSIDE! MORE MHUC THAN EVER BEFORE!
OOH-OOH! CAN I GET A SELFIE? AND CAN YOU MAKE IT LOOK REAL SCARY?
WHY NOT? JUST DON'T ASK ME TO SAY "BLEH-BLEH-BLEH."
I MEAN, WHAT IS THAT, ANYWAY?
THE INSIDIOUS CLING MOVES ABOUT THE CONFERENCE, THE HELPFUL MONSTERS UNAWARE OF HIS TRUE GOALS!
NOW THAT I HAVE MY "EVIDENCE" I'LL POST IT EVERYWHERE!
HOTEL TRANSYLVANIA
WELCOME!
EVERYWHERE!
HA-HA-HA-HA!

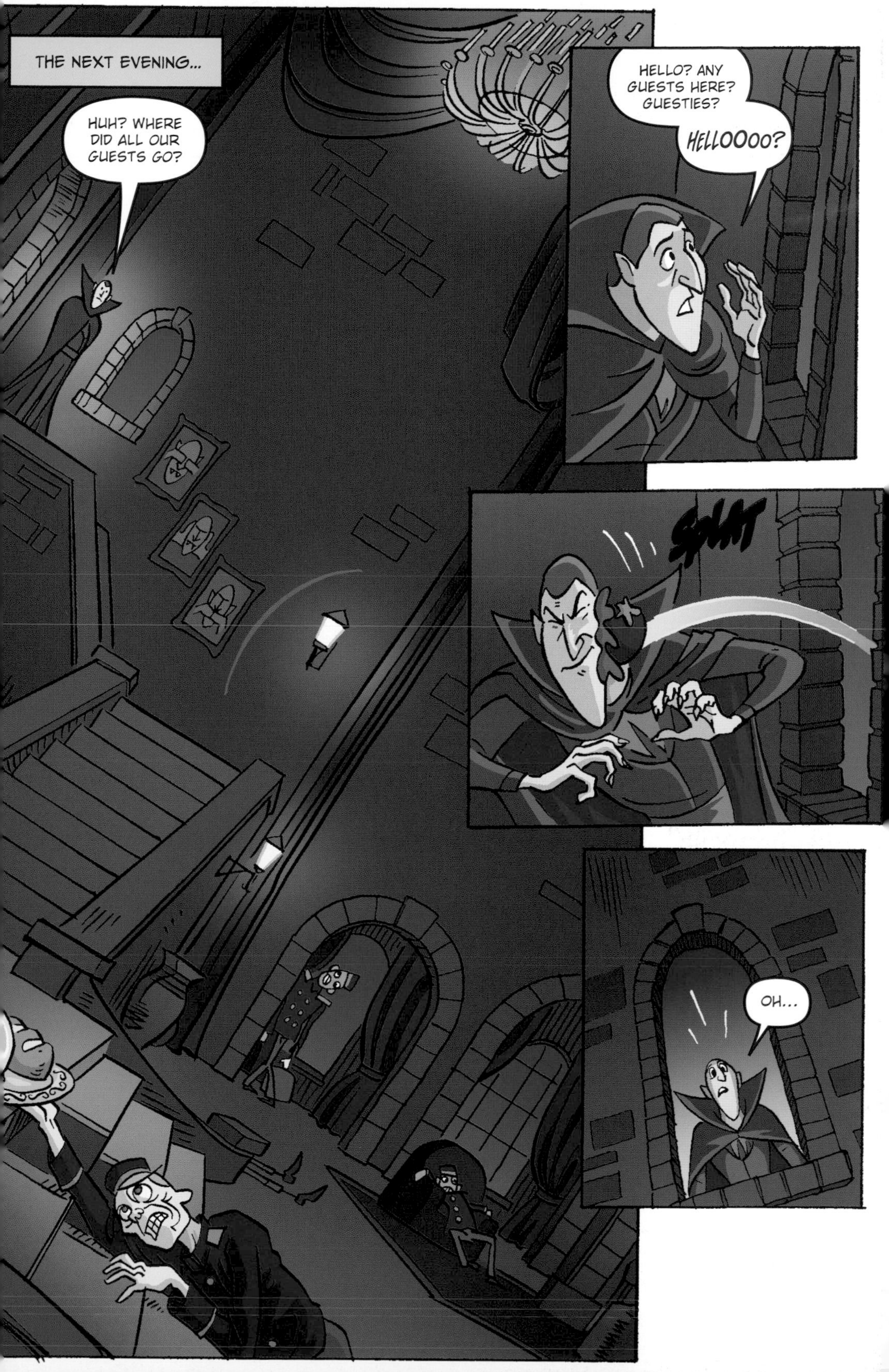
THE NEXT EVENING...
HUH? WHERE DID ALL OUR GUESTS GO?
HELLO? ANY GUESTS HERE? GUESTIES?
HELLOOOo?
SPLAT
OH...

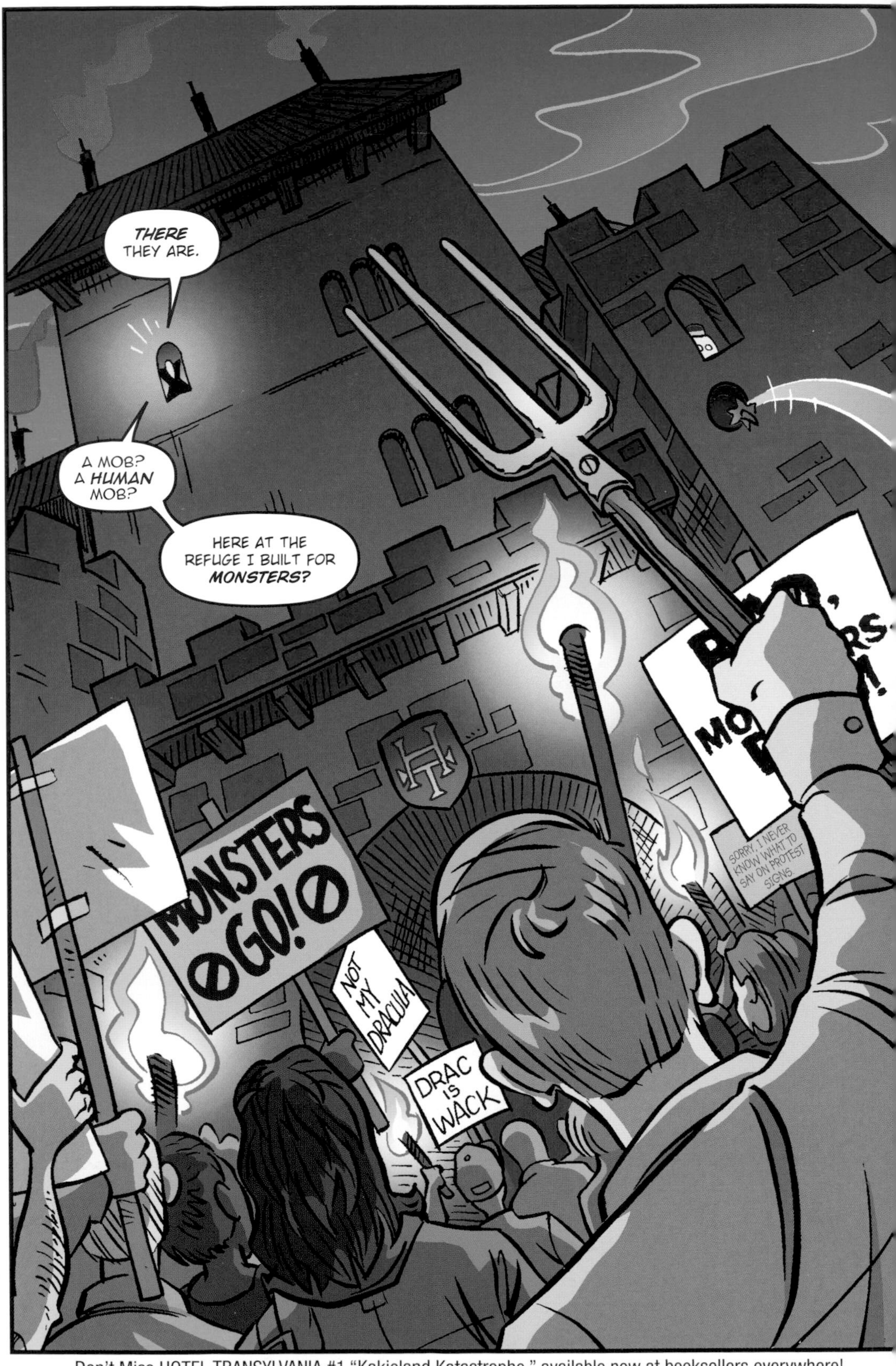

THERE THEY ARE.
A MOB? A ***HUMAN*** MOB?
HERE AT THE REFUGE I BUILT FOR ***MONSTERS?***
MONSTERS GO!
NOT MY DRACULA
DRAC IS WACK
SORRY, I NEVER KNOW WHAT TO SAY ON PROTEST SIGNS.

Special Preview of DINOSAURS #1 "In the Beginning…" by Plumeri & Bloz…

TYRANNOSAURUS REX

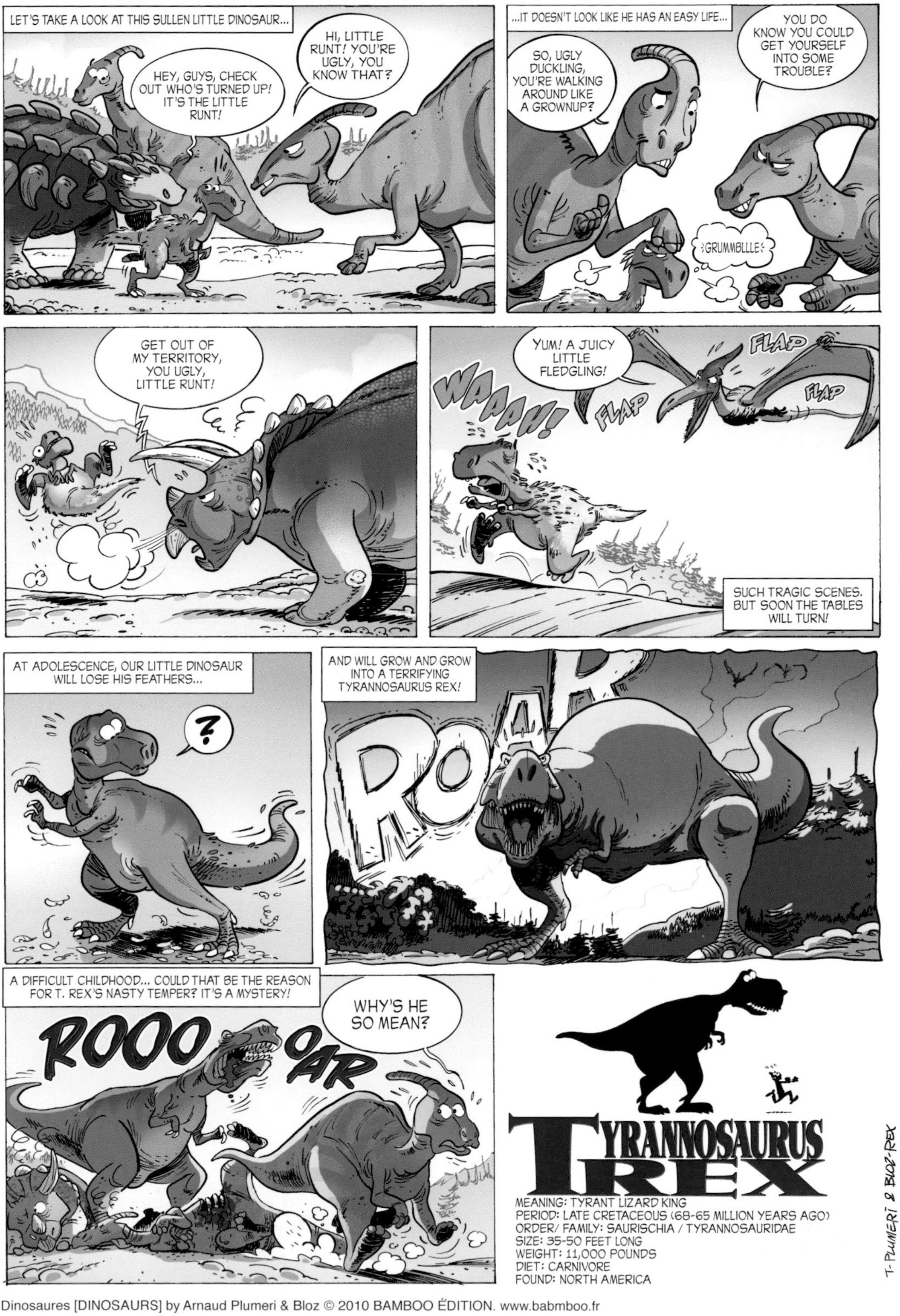
LET'S TAKE A LOOK AT THIS SULLEN LITTLE DINOSAUR...
HEY, GUYS, CHECK OUT WHO'S TURNED UP! IT'S THE LITTLE RUNT!
HI, LITTLE RUNT! YOU'RE UGLY, YOU KNOW THAT?
...IT DOESN'T LOOK LIKE HE HAS AN EASY LIFE...
SO, UGLY DUCKLING, YOU'RE WALKING AROUND LIKE A GROWNUP?
YOU DO KNOW YOU COULD GET YOURSELF INTO SOME TROUBLE?
GRUMMBLLLE
GET OUT OF MY TERRITORY, YOU UGLY, LITTLE RUNT!
YUM! A JUICY LITTLE FLEDGLING!
FLAP
FLAP
FLAP
WAAAAH!
SUCH TRAGIC SCENES. BUT SOON THE TABLES WILL TURN!
AT ADOLESCENCE, OUR LITTLE DINOSAUR WILL LOSE HIS FEATHERS...
?
AND WILL GROW AND GROW INTO A TERRIFYING TYRANNOSAURUS REX!
ROAR
A DIFFICULT CHILDHOOD... COULD THAT BE THE REASON FOR T. REX'S NASTY TEMPER? IT'S A MYSTERY!
ROOOOAR
WHY'S HE SO MEAN?
TYRANNOSAURUS REX
MEANING: TYRANT LIZARD KING
PERIOD: LATE CRETACEOUS (68-65 MILLION YEARS AGO)
ORDER/ FAMILY: SAURISCHIA / TYRANNOSAURIDAE
SIZE: 35-50 FEET LONG
WEIGHT: 11,000 POUNDS
DIET: CARNIVORE
FOUND: NORTH AMERICA
T-PLUMERI & BLOZ-REX

TRICERATOPS

HMMM... I SHOULD MAKE A MEAL OF THAT *TRICERATOPS!*

ARE YOU CRAZY? HAVE YOU SEEN THAT BEAST?

WITH ITS POWERFUL PHYSIQUE, IT CAN DESTROY EVERYTHING IN ITS PATH.

CRUNCH GRUNCH YUM...

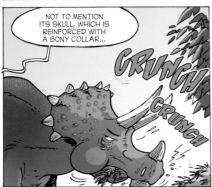

NOT TO MENTION ITS SKULL, WHICH IS REINFORCED WITH A BONY COLLAR...

CRUNCH CRUNCH

AND WORST OF ALL: THREE HORNS THAT ARE SHARP AS KNIVES!

;SNIFF!;

?

I KNOW ALL THAT! BUT IT'S SO GOOD, AND SUPER PRACTICAL FOR EATING!

SUPER PRACTICAL?

EEEK!

ROAR

OWIE! *ROAR* YUM ARGH! GROW OOW! CRUMP

WELL, YES, SUPER PRACTICAL: YOU DONT JUST GET THE MEAT: IT ALSO COMES WITH TOOTHPICKS!

DELICIOUS!

;SLURP;

SCRATCH! SCRATCH!

CRUNCH

YUM...

CRUNCH

TRICERATOPS

MEANING: THREE-HORNED FACE
PERIOD: LATE CRETACEOUS (68-65 MILLION YEARS AGO)
ORDER/ FAMILY: ORNITHISCHIA/ CERATOPSIDAE
SIZE: 30 FEET LONG
WEIGHT: 20,000 LBS.
DIET: HERBIVORE
FOUND: NORTH AMERICA

AT HOME WITH THE PTEROSAURS

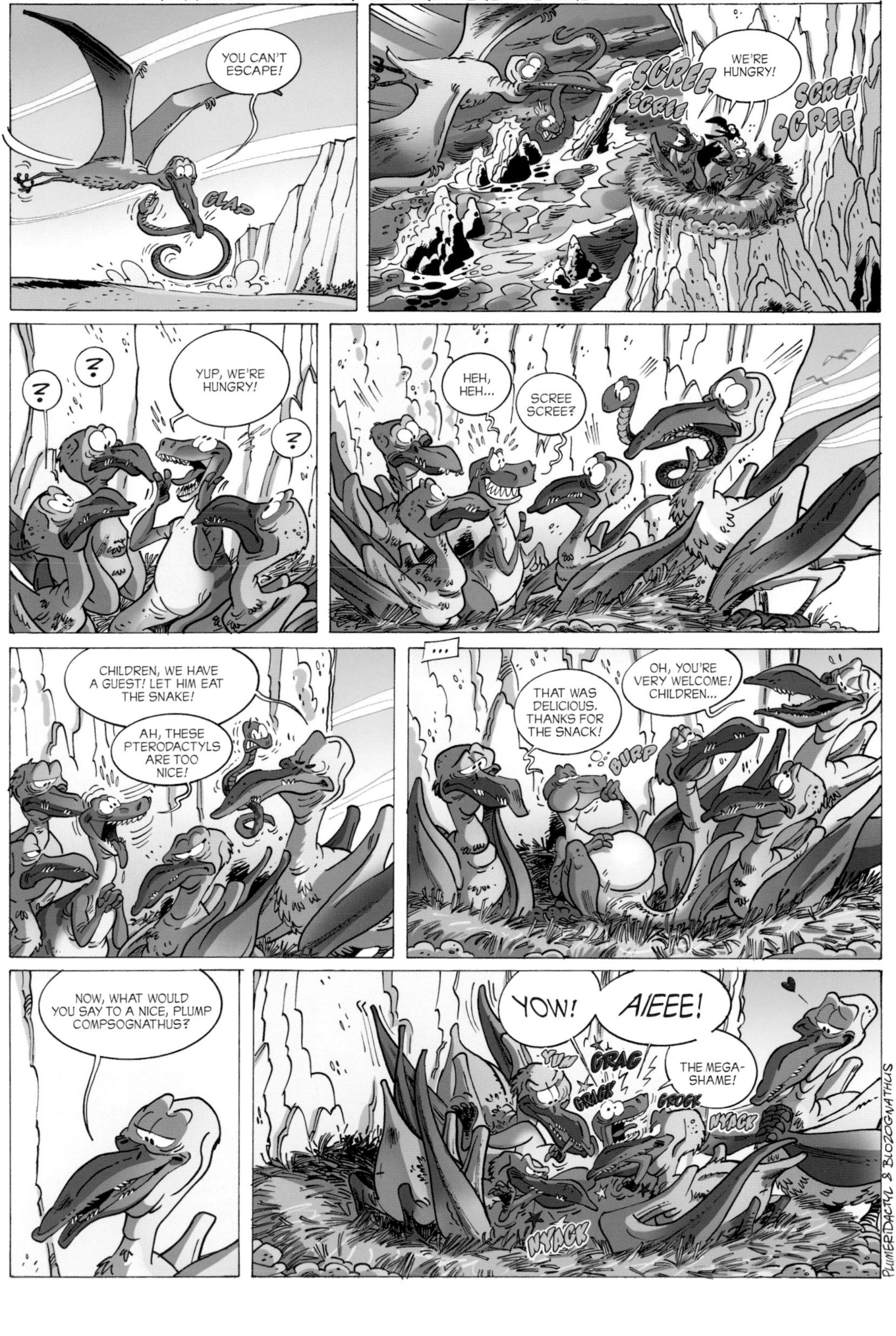

YOU CAN'T ESCAPE!
CLAP
SCREE
SCREE
WE'RE HUNGRY!
SCREE
SCREE
?
?
YUP, WE'RE HUNGRY!
?
HEH, HEH...
SCREE SCREE?
CHILDREN, WE HAVE A GUEST! LET HIM EAT THE SNAKE!
AH, THESE PTERODACTYLS ARE TOO NICE!
...
THAT WAS DELICIOUS. THANKS FOR THE SNACK!
OH, YOU'RE VERY WELCOME! CHILDREN...
BURP
NOW, WHAT WOULD YOU SAY TO A NICE, PLUMP COMPSOGNATHUS?
YOW!
AIEEE!
YUM
CRAC
CRACK
CROCK
THE MEGA-SHAME!
NYACK
NYACK
PLUMERIDACTYL & BLOZOGNATHUS

VELOCIRAPTOR

ONCE UPON A TIME, THERE WAS A SLIGHTLY STUPID *PROTOCERATOPS*...

THE DROMAESAURIDS! THE DROMAESAURIDS!

SAY WHAT? SAY WHO? WHY? YOU'RE LEAVING?

...WHO DIDN'T KNOW THAT THE MOST FAMOUS *DROMAESAURIDS* WERE...

RAPTORS!

HE DISCOVERED THEIR FAVORITE WEAPON RIGHT AWAY!...

HOLY COW! YOU DON'T CUT YOUR TOENAILS OFTEN ENOUGH!

VGH!

AND THEIR FAVORITE WAY OF CHASING: STALKING...

PUFF...

GO AWAY!

PUFF... HELP!

PUFF...

...TO EXHAUSTION!

THAT'S GOOD! HE'S DONE FOR-- LET'S EAT!

ONCE UPON A TIME, THERE WERE SOME SLIGHTLY STUPID *VELOCIRAPTORS*...

?   ?   ?

..WHO DISCOVERED THAT *TARBOSAURUS* WAS A LAZY GUY.

NO FAIR! WE DID ALL THE WORK!

SSANKS, DUDES!

GIVE US BACK OUR MEAT!

VELOCIRAPTOR

MEANING: SWIFT THIEF
PERIOD: LATE CRETACEOUS (75-70 MILLION YEARS AGO)
ORDER/ FAMILY: SAURISCHIA/ DROMAEOSAURIDAE
SIZE: 7 FEET LONG
WEIGHT: 30 LBS.
DIET: CARNIVORE
FOUND: MONGOLIA, CHINA

PLUIRAPTOR 2 BUCOCERATOPS

DINOSAURS #1 "In the Beginning…" is available at booksellers everywhere.